A DASH OF SCOT
DISTINGUISHED SCOTS

ELIZA KNIGHT

KNIGHT
MEDIA

ABOUT THE BOOK

Jane Austen's world meets the Highlands of Scotland in an exciting new, sexy Scottish Regency series by USA Today *bestselling author Eliza Knight. Gently bred ladies collide with noble Scottish heroes in these new dramatic and emotionally charged tales of misadventure and love.*

Sensible Poppy Featherstone has always known that her duty would be to marry well, for her younger sister Anise is capricious and romantic. Yet Poppy longs for a happy ever after, a true union of like minds. She thought she'd found just that in Dougal Mackay, the Earl of Reay, a relative of her sister-in-law. Yet after he scandalously kisses her in a private garden, he flees, leaving her alone with no explanation for a year. Then, the sudden death of their father forces Poppy and Anise to rely on the charity of family members, moving them to the townhouse of their half-brother. Grief-stricken, Poppy prepares to endure the change as she has everything else in life: with grace and logic.

When Dougal finds out that Poppy is staying at his sister's house, he rushes there. He's never been able to forget her, and he vows to help Poppy and her family through this difficult time. Except when Dougal was nineteen, he entered into a fool's bargain: if he were not married by twenty-nine, he would wed the young lass he'd just met in the drinking hall. Dougal never thought the woman would take him seriously—until he gets a letter that she's coming to Edinburgh and expects him to honor the terms of their drunken agreement. Dougal's heart belongs to Poppy, but his honor may force him to wed another.

Just as Poppy discovers Dougal's apparent engagement, her family is forced to relocate again, this time to a small country village. Dougal is determined not to let her go. They might still have a chance if he can convince Poppy to wed him before his twenty-ninth birthday. Ultimately, it is not sense that may save their romance, but sensibility.

The Conquered Bride Series

Conquered by the Highlander
Seduced by the Laird
Taken by the Highlander (a Conquered bride novella)
Claimed by the Warrior
Stolen by the Laird
Protected by the Laird (a Conquered bride novella)
Guarded by the Warrior

The MacDougall Legacy Series

Laird of Shadows
Laird of Twilight
Laird of Darkness

Pirates of Britannia: Devils of the Deep

Savage of the Sea
The Sea Devil
A Pirate's Bounty

THE THISTLES AND ROSES SERIES

Promise of a Knight
Eternally Bound
Breath from the Sea

The Highland Bound Series (Erotic time-travel)

Behind the Plaid
Bared to the Laird

Dark Side of the Laird
Highlander's Touch
Highlander Undone
Highlander Unraveled

Touchstone Series

Highland Steam
Highland Brawn
Highland Tryst
Highland Heat

Wicked Women

Her Desperate Gamble
Seducing the Sheriff
Kiss Me, Cowboy

☙❧

HISTORICAL FICTION

The Mayfair Bookshop

Releasing June 6, 2023
The Other Astaire

Tales From the Tudor Court

My Lady Viper
Prisoner of the Queen

Ancient Historical Fiction

A Day of Fire: a novel of Pompeii
A Year of Ravens: a novel of Boudica's Rebellion

French Revolution

Ribbons of Scarlet: a novel of the French Revolution

☙❧

AUGUST 2024

Cover Design by Dar Albert

Edited by Erica Monroe

KNIGHT
MEDIA

PROLOGUE

Moonlight lit the path as they ran, hand in hand, giggling like adolescents through the garden maze.

Miss Poppy Featherstone had never done anything like this before. And if her mother or father knew she was doing it now, they would grab her by the other hand and yank her back to reality.

But fortunately, she and Dougal Mackay, the Earl of Reay, had been discreet when they'd gone out onto the balcony for fresh air. Discreet as they slipped into the shadows of said balcony. Discreet as they sneaked down the stairs to find the elusive statue in the garden that had supposedly been made in their host's great-grandfather's likeness, including the protruding codpiece he insisted on wearing.

The entire adventure was scandalous.

If discovered, she'd be banished from society—that was for certain. But Poppy didn't care. What Poppy wanted was to be alone with Dougal Mackay. To listen to his jests and tease him back. To hear him whisper about things no one ever told a lady, like the statue.

Her friends were so preoccupied with finding husbands that they wouldn't notice she was gone. Her sister was home tucked up in bed, pouting at being a year too young to attend a ball. Mama was off gossiping with her friends, and Papa was drinking brandy with his Parliament cronies in a corner.

That meant Poppy wasn't likely to be missed, at least not for a little while, and if she needed to, she could always hail a hackney and disappear into the night with a footman letting her parents know she'd gone home due to some fictional ailment.

But for now, she wanted to concentrate on Dougal Mackay, the Earl of Reay, and his strong, firm hand holding hers. The crunch of the gravelly path beneath her slippers, the cool night air on her heated face.

"'Tis just around this corner, I swear it," Lord Reay said.

"That's what you said about the last corner."

"It has been nearly a decade since I've seen it. Do ye suppose they've taken it down?"

"I dearly hope not. I was very much looking forward to seeing it."

"Which part, my lady?"

Poppy laughed because his teasing was so raw, so real, so unfettered. Everyone in society was always tiptoeing around the right things to say. But not Dougal. He said what he was thinking and observing, and she liked that.

They'd known each other a couple of years, but it was only this season she'd caught his attention. Already they'd danced and danced at every ball they could.

Tonight was the first time he'd invited her onto the balcony for air, a place where most people went to receive a kiss. But he'd not kissed her. She'd thought he might, but he kept looking toward the garden maze. Enough so that she'd actually turned around to see what he found so fascinating, which was when he'd imparted to her that he'd witnessed firsthand the scandalous statue.

They came to another dead end, and Dougal stopped. He ran a hand through his dark hair, looking perplexed.

"All right, I'll give ye a boost, and ye see if ye can see the statue's head."

"A boost?"

"Aye." Dougal dropped to one knee and patted his other knee. "Step here, pretend I am a stool."

She wanted to tell him he was a rather handsome stool. Impossibly tall with muscles she wanted to squeeze.

"All right, but if you drop me, we'll have to come up with a proper excuse. My mother would become apoplectic to learn I'd stepped on you."

Dougal chuckled. "I promise." He slapped his thigh just above his knee. "Now step."

Poppy pressed a hand into his thick shoulder and squeezed as she placed her foot on his strong thigh and hoisted herself up. She wavered slightly, and Dougal grasped her on the bum.

"Oh," she gasped.

"Sorry," he said with a chuckle. "I didna mean to grab ye there."

Oh, but she didn't mind. He resituated his hand at her calf, and even that was scandalous and delicious all at once.

"Do ye see anything?" he asked, pulling her back from all the thoughts swirling in her head from his touch.

Poppy peered over the garden hedge and wondered if anyone back on the balcony of the London manse would notice. She could certainly make out their shadows, but thankfully, she couldn't discern any faces, which meant she was likely in the clear.

Across the hedges, all she saw were rows and twists and turns of more hedges. "Not a single marble head," she said.

"That's disappointing. We'll have to continue our search."

"I suppose we will." She looked one more time to be sure, but there wasn't anything that resembled a statue, only foliage and air.

Poppy started to step down but wobbled and then lost her balance. Dougal's reflexes saved her from a hard landing in the gravel, his arms catching her around her back, her bottom landing on his still-propped thigh, and she grasped hold of him around his shoulders.

Their faces were close. The moon reflected in his eyes the color of the night sky.

"I'm so clumsy. Thank you for catching me," she managed to say.

"It wouldna do for a lady to land on the ground. Ye might ruin your dress." His brogue was raspier than usual, and his eyes skimmed down to her mouth.

Neither of them made a move to let the other go. Poppy licked her lower lip, hoping for the kiss she'd thought she was going to get on the balcony. She and Dougal had a real connection, one she thought might very well lead to a proposal. It wasn't as if men were lining up to propose, and daring the think that Dougal might—perhaps that was the most unsensible thing she'd ever done in her life. And Dougal Mackay ticked off all the boxes on the list she'd made last year.

Charming.
Funny.
Handsome.
Strong.
Scottish.
Not dull.

Kind.

But most importantly, he had lips made for kissing, and after spending much of her adolescence reading romance novels, she was ready to find a man who swept her off her feet.

And then his mouth was on hers. A soft brush of his lips, and she sighed into his kiss. His lips were warm, velvet as they pressed to hers. His breath fanned softly over her cheek. For all she'd imagined a first kiss to be, this was it, the moment she'd been waiting for. And it was heaven.

Dougal lifted his face away for a moment, staring into her eyes, imploring, questioning. And she did the only thing she could think of—where her hands rested at the nape of his neck, she nudged, urging him back to her mouth.

"Ye..." was all he said before he pressed his lips to hers again. Only this time, the softness melted into heat.

His tongue swiped the seam of her lips, and she parted on a gasp. That subtle opening had his tongue slipping inside to slide wickedly and deliciously across her own. My goodness, she didn't know this was possible in a kiss. Tongues...so decadent. She'd never be able to eat or drink or lick her lips without thinking of this moment, of Dougal Mackay.

And maybe she wouldn't have to. For if he'd invited her out to this garden, danced with her at ball after ball, and now was kissing her, then certainly this meant he wanted her to be his wife.

Knowing that a proposal was forthcoming only heightened her excitement—her desire—and she leaned into his kiss, boldly copying the swipes and licks and nibbles.

The spicy, earthy scent of him surrounded her, doing something wild to her senses. Everything inside of her seemed to come alive with a tingling heat that increased until her skin felt like it was afire and only his touch could put out the flames. Except they blazed hotter.

This was wicked and oh, so very scandalous. If anyone were to see them... she'd be ruined forever. Oh, who was she trying to fool? The moment his lips had touched hers, she was done for. She was powerless to make herself stop.

And so, she kept on kissing him, finding a home in his arms and the pleasure he wrought on her mouth. If he were to ask her right then and there, she'd let him own her completely. Dougal Mackay was, without a doubt, the most captivating, intoxicating man she'd ever met.

Dougal deepened the kiss, passion and desire fueling them both, but when she whimpered from some place in the back of her throat where inhibition had taken over, Dougal pulled away. He stared into her bemused gaze with hooded eyes that bespoke of desire. His lips were as wet and swollen as hers felt. The two of them were equally ravished by a kiss that had devoured them whole, body and soul.

"My lady," he murmured.

"Poppy."

"I'm sorry," he said, the desire on his face seconds ago evaporating into something akin to...fear?

That couldn't be right. Why was he afraid? His kiss had been divine...

"You don't have to be sorry."

He shook his head. And in a move so deft it was as if he'd practiced it a thousand times, he stood with her in his arms and stepped away.

"I shouldna have done that. Ye...we..." He ran his hands through his hair, and she felt uneasy.

The heat centered in her belly turned as cold as ice. Was he...rejecting her?

"What's wrong?" she asked. "A moment ago..."

But she didn't want to give voice to the fun they'd had as they ran through the maze, the fantasy of his kiss dissolving as if a dream she had awoken from as he turned his back and walked—nay, *ran*—away from her.

Mortification took hold, and all Poppy could do was stare dumbfounded at the man—her dream, her future—as he disappeared from view and her life.

Edinburgh, one year later...

S itting on the stiff and scratchy cushion of the window seat, Poppy stared out the paned glass at the dismal, foggy morning.

The last of their stuffed trunks had been brought inside her half-brother's house in Edinburgh, where she, her mother and her sister had begged for the charity of a roof over their heads. Quite unfair, it all was. Less than a month before, she'd never wanted for a thing, and now, they were practically paupers.

Edward did not share the same father as Poppy and her sister Anise, their mother having remarried after losing her first husband—Edward's father, Lord Leven. And now their mother had been made a widow again, and Poppy and Anise mourned greatly the loss of their gentle father.

The situation had become quite bleak when their father fell ill suddenly and relayed the succession of his house and wealth. The majority of which did not fall to them at all. Even their mother seemed surprised by this. Their house, the great and beautiful Featherstone Park, had been entailed to a male heir, which didn't fall to Edward's shoulders given he was no blood relation to George Featherstone, Baron Cullen. A meager one hundred pounds a year split between the three of them would mean remaining frugal and relying on the charity of others, not something Poppy was certain her sister would be able to accomplish, as Anise loved shopping for new linens and fabrics and already had a wardrobe fit for a princess.

Their father had ensured that their dowries would remain in trust until they married—but that money would transfer to a husband and did nothing to help with their current living situation.

For a week, they'd tried to live with their cousin, but the circumstances had been abysmal, and he'd treated them more like servants than anything else.

They hardly knew their cousin, Thomas, who'd come from somewhere north, the exact location never mentioned, and then completely overtaken the house. His wife had treated them like the staff, going so far as to pawn off their five insufferable children onto Poppy and Anise's shoulders, encouraging Mother to get her hands deep into the kitchen pots, and complaining about everything in the household that their mother had worked hard to create.

After a week of Thomas's family making them miserable, her mother had arranged for them to leave the only home that Poppy had ever known to live with Edward in the city.

But the situation at Edward's was, perhaps not surprisingly, very different. His wife resented their presence and wasn't very good at hiding the fact. Poppy believed she actually practiced the cruel jibes before letting them out as they were so...exacting in their precision to cut through one's emotions and bury themselves in the heart.

"What are you doing perched there? You're going to ruin your dress." As if on cue, her sister-in-law marched into the drawing room with her nasal, whiney voice, in a dress far too ostentatious in its frills and flounces for daywear and pointed a long finger at Poppy.

If Poppy squinted her eyes just so, that long, accusing finger grew blurry and took on the crooked, wretched look of a witch's talon.

Poppy pressed her lips together, her fingers splayed on the cover of a book she'd yet had the energy to open—so unlike her—and tried to find a suitable response. She didn't exactly care about her dress as she wasn't expecting company and thought merely to wallow in self-pity today.

"Did you hear me?"

Poppy would have liked to continue pretending that she did not hear her sister-in-law because that would have made her feel better, but the rising pitch of Mary's voice was such that if she didn't respond soon, she was sure to hear it from Edward later, who would end his tirade with "Why can't you be more like Mary?"

If Poppy had to hear that one more time, she might lose her mind and be sent off to Bedlam, at which point her sister and mother would truly be in a pile of it then, given Poppy seemed to be the most rational of the three.

They'd not even had a night here, and Edward had said it once already. Every time she came to visit, he made the remark, which she found odd, considering Mary was the one harping on everyone while Poppy hardly said a thing.

After having her coming out season the year before being relegated to the life of a guest in someone else's house and essentially labeled a pauper, not that anyone would say such to her face—except Mary—was the embarrassment of Poppy's life. And it was accompanied by the grief of her life too.

She missed her father something awful.

Which meant she merely wanted to curl up into a ball and pretend she was anyone other than Miss Poppy Featherstone.

Mary had yet to lose either parent. Not that she struck Poppy as the type to be empathetic even if she had experienced such devastation. More like she'd dust her hands as soon as the coffin lid closed.

"Good morning, Mary." Poppy kept her tone as sweet as syrup and smiled in the same manner, hoping to ease her sister-in-law's ire. If only she could find the pin stuck under her skin and pluck it out. Mary seemed to be one constantly suffering.

Mary's brow wrinkled that she'd not been formally addressed, but Poppy didn't care. She was too exhausted trying to please the one person in the house she'd thought she might befriend besides her own sister. A thought that had been dashed about thirty seconds upon entry.

Their mother was far too inside her own grief to be of any comfort.

Anise took that moment to enter the drawing room, too, her face drawn. She headed toward the piano, settling on the bench, her fingers poised over the keys. She took a dramatic breath and started playing Beethoven's "Sonata," the keys and notes filled with such sorrow that Mary actually groaned like a petulant toddler.

"Will you both quit your moping?" Mary's arms flailed with exasperation. "The atmosphere is far too funereal for me."

Shocked, Anise's hands fell flat on the keys in a wretched sound, her mouth agape as she stared. During the silence that passed for the next fifteen seconds, Poppy could hear the creaks of the house, the carriages rolling on the cobbles outside, and the beat of her heart in muted tones as if she'd been forced into a bubble and every sound was on the outside of it.

Poppy dropped her book, unable to hide her flinch. "Our father has just passed," Poppy said. "You might be more considerate in your word choices and in your attitude."

She regretted the words as soon as they were out of her mouth. Mary's lips curled, and she was certain there was about to be a huge rebuke. But a swift knock on the drawing room door had them all quiet and attention on the butler, who was opening the door and announcing that Lord Dougal Mackay was present.

Poppy bounced to stand, smoothing a hand down her skirt.

Dougal Mackay.

They'd met first at Edward and Mary's wedding several years prior. And then again, last year at a ball in London, he'd swept her off her feet and broken her heart. Back when life seemed easy and grand and her future bright.

To see him now sent a rush of embarrassing heat through her, taking her right back to that ball where he'd danced with her, making her feel as if she were the only woman in the room. And outside, in the garden maze shadows, he'd pulled her in for a kiss that made her toes curl in her slippers until he'd abruptly run away.

If only there'd been at least one other proposal for her hand in marriage she'd not find herself in this situation. But she'd put all her faith in waiting for Dougal to bend down on one knee, not paying attention to any other suitors. But his offer had never come, and he'd abruptly left London for Scotland, and she'd been without a proposal of marriage or any prospects.

When she herself had returned to Scotland, she'd been hopeful for a reunion, but she'd not seen him since, even though she'd looked.

The Earl of Reay sauntered into the room, the very picture of a hero—tall and lithe, his magnetism drawing the eye of all three ladies. He swept off his hat, bent his lofty body in a bow and straightened, a teasing smile on his impossibly perfect mouth. His dark hair was swept over his brow in a way that looked as if he'd just ridden here at a pace that would set Poppy's heart pounding, giving him both a casual and dangerous appearance.

"Dougal, we weren't expecting you this morning." Mary cast her gaze over her brother in a very judgmental way, which Poppy found infuriating.

It was extremely unfortunate for the two of them to be related. As in love with him as Poppy thought she was, she kept waiting for the curtain to drop, and he would reveal himself as harsh and cold as Mary. Even after he'd left London without a word, she'd still held out hope to see him and couldn't fault him for whatever reason that had called him away. As much as it hurt not to have seen him in nearly a year, she also couldn't cease the flutter of her belly, the squeeze of her heart, and that smile... He and Mary were too impossibly different for her even to consider they shared blood.

The man was every bit as handsome now as he was the previous times she'd been in his presence. The cut of his breeches showed off the muscles of his legs. His starched shirt was impeccable, and his jacket, spread over his broad shoulders, had the shiniest black buttons.

Dougal ignored his sister's rebuke and nodded toward Anise before settling his dark eyes on Poppy. "Ladies, 'tis a gorgeous day, and I thought I might offer to escort ye on a carriage ride around the city." Dougal's Scottish brogue was stronger than his sister's by far. Likely because Mary had spent much time in London perfecting the aristocratic accent of the ton, whereas he had preferred the Highlands.

Anise and Poppy had also spent much of their time in London in their youth, never truly developing a strong brogue either.

"Gorgeous?" Mary frowned and glanced outside at the dreary atmosphere; her puckered brow pinched enough that the sky might cry for her.

"Well, we can make it a gorgeous day can we no'? Or at least pretend?" Dougal winked at Poppy.

Something inside her chest cracked. Why was he so different from his sister? Kind, sweet, funny, as if when they were born, the pleasant half of one's personality went to Dougal and the unpleasant parts were saved for Mary. And why was he acting as though a year hadn't passed since the last time that they'd seen each other—since he'd kissed away her ability to breathe and see sense? Since he'd abandoned her without a word, taking her hopes with him.

She couldn't exactly say he'd dashed them or stomped on them; it was more like he'd taken her hopes and tied them up in a nice, neat bow and stuck them in his pocket for safe-keeping.

"No, you cannot. That's rubbish. This weather is not good for the skin," Mary concluded, dismissing her brother with a wave of her taloned fingers.

"I'll go." Poppy made imploring eyes at Anise as it wouldn't be proper for her to go alone.

Anise looked slightly petulant, only wanting to remain behind and play out the rest of the sonata before spilling another bucket of tears into her pillow. As much as she empathized with her sister, for she'd been on the verge of doing just that before Mary came in to prod her, Poppy also knew it was best for her sister to get some fresh air and have a little bit of amusement, if only to distract her a moment from her grief.

Poppy didn't stop begging with her eyes. She contemplated outright saying the advantages of the ride, but Mary's nearly bared teeth kept her from speaking. Dougal seemed to have picked up on her desperation, for he approached Anise at the piano.

"Come get some air, my lady. The sonata will be here when we return, and perhaps the grayness of Edinburgh will add a certain note to your playing."

How was it that he could say the most perfect things?

Anise glanced up at Dougal, blinking as she processed his suggestion for melancholic inspiration, and then she nodded in agreement.

Poppy breathed out a sigh of relief. She needed to get out of this house. Away from Mary. Away from the dreariness of mourning. And she understood the irony of escaping the dreary house for a dreary, cloudy day, but perhaps the thick air would do something to make her feel better after all. If anything, it would get her away from Mary and her deep desire to scratch her sister-in-law's eyes out.

Dougal took both their arms, and Mary's eye roll could have been felt in London. Poppy wouldn't have been surprised if she'd caused the earth to quake in some far-off continent.

"Do be back in time for tea," Mary advised. "We've several ladies calling, and it wouldn't do for you not to be present." Her words were not directed at anyone in particular but felt by all three, as evidenced by the knowing glances they passed.

Mary practically hissed at the three of them having a bonding moment.

That was hours from now. Where exactly did she think Dougal was going to take them on their carriage ride? Down to London?

Dougal, his voice as calm as one of the lochs on a summer day, said, "I'll be sure to have them back in plenty of time for tea. Am I invited?"

"No," Mary retorted venomously, her mouth turned down, but rather than be offended, Dougal laughed as if he were used to his sister's disposition.

Poppy wasn't certain she'd ever be used to Mary. Her acerbic tones and puckered features made it look as if she had a lemon rind in her mouth and a dog's mess on her shoes.

"Shame," Dougal said, though he didn't sound too upset about it; in fact, it was the opposite.

If Poppy had the option to be disinvited to tea, she'd feel the same way: happy as a salmon swimming upstream.

Mary muttered something under her breath and then took up her place at the piano, playing a tune fit for a party rather than the melancholy of her sisters-in-law who'd recently lost their father.

Poppy tugged on Dougal's arm, and he hurried them out of the drawing room without so much as a backward glance. Good riddance.

They donned their coats in the foyer and then proceeded outside where Dougal's curricle sat as if it had been waiting for them, the top lowered to allow the passengers fresh air and a view of their surroundings. As if he'd swept into the house to swish them away from their misery, escaping his sister being the plan all along.

The coolness of autumn bit through Poppy's sleeves, and

gooseflesh rose on her right arm; her left quite cozy in the crook of Dougal's hold.

"Please accept my apologies for my sister," he said as a footman opened the door to the open curricle and put down the steps for them to climb in.

Dougal actually looked sad about it, and Poppy felt bad for him, knowing he'd had to grow up with Mary. That had not been easy, she was certain. She and Anise had, of course, had their rows and didn't always see eye to eye, but in the end, they were at least kind to each other.

Poppy glanced up at the sky, a mist threatening to come down on them.

"I've umbrellas should the sky decide to ruin our day," Dougal said.

"Thank you."

Poppy climbed into the curricle, her sister sitting beside her and Dougal opposite them. He wasn't a bad view to have to watch the whole ride through. She rather liked looking at him. Which was a scandalous thing to think. What lady of good breeding would stare unabashedly at a handsome man?

She supposed she wasn't a lady of good breeding then, though her mother might throw a fit to hear her think it.

And also unfortunate, given he'd left without a word for nearly a year, and there was every possibility he would do so again. She had no stake on him. A kiss in a garden. A enough dances to make her believe he'd set his intentions.

But that kiss...it had been exquisite and left a mark on her that no other man was likely to erase. And yet, he'd walked away. As if kissing her had been the same as picking up the morning paper. Easily gone through and discarded without a need to review again.

The only thing she currently had going for her was that

she resided in his sister's house. That meant she was likely to see him more often than not.

Dougal handed each of them a wool tartan blanket to place over their laps. "In case you catch a chill."

"Thank you, my lord," Poppy said as she spread it over her legs, instantly feeling the warmth of the wool blocking the autumn chill. "For the blanket and for offering to take us about."

"My pleasure." He glanced at the massive Edinburgh townhouse, which hid the tyrant he called sister. "I know how stuffy it can be when ye're all cooped up. And Mary is...not the best company sometimes." He grinned mischievously at Poppy and Anise as if they shared in some joke. Sadly, Mary's attitude was not funny. "If ye tell her I said that I'll deny it."

"We wouldn't dare." Poppy laughed softly, feeling marginally better.

"You both are so different," Anise pointed out without hesitation. "How do you suppose that is?"

Poppy stared at her sister, shocked she'd voice such a question, even if it were something she'd been contemplating forever. Dougal chuckled at Anise's bold question, and Poppy let out a breath. She had her ideas about their differences but waited for what Dougal might have to say.

"My sister is the eldest." He shrugged. "She has always had a heap of responsibility placed on her, and I suppose she takes it *verra* seriously."

"Very." Anise nodded seriously. "*Very,* very."

"For example, her tea parties," Dougal said. "No male would ever be invited."

"Why's that?" Anise asked.

"It's a henpecking, I'm certain."

Poppy frowned. She wasn't certain she was going to enjoy

sitting around with a dozen Marys while they complained about the men in their lives.

"Perhaps we'll be late for tea," Poppy teased, the first time she'd done so in ages.

"I could direct our driver to take us over to Skye. Ye'd be certain to miss it then."

"I wouldn't mind," Poppy teased.

"We'd be gone for days." Anise clapped and abruptly stopped. "But Mama would go mad."

"Alas, I'd likely be set upon by the gatekeepers of society for having absconded with two beautiful ladies."

Poppy's face heated in a blush. The majority of abscondings ended in marriage, and she was irritated with herself for that being her first thought: she wouldn't mind being absconded with by him.

She stared hard at her fingers folded neatly in her lap as if they were the most interesting thing in this curricle and not the man opposite her, but then she chanced a glance up at Dougal. He was watching her, his expression thoughtful.

If Anise weren't here, she might have been bold enough to ask what he was thinking. But alas, she wasn't willing to risk her sister tattling to their mother later about her obvious interest in the man. Not if she wanted Dougal Mackay to come back.

A year without seeing him—hearing him—had been painful enough as it was.

He was the first bright spot in an endless sea of literal and figurative gray days. She wasn't going to do anything to ruin that.

"We wouldn't want to be the reason you were banished," Poppy offered instead. "Not when you've tossed us a lifeline."

Dougal smiled at her, his expression soft and endearing

and confusing. He bent in a mock bow. "I'm at your service, my lady."

2

Dougal Mackay was very aware of the two inches of space between his massive knee and the knee of the lady who sat opposite him in a dark gray wool coat with blue-and-white plaid cuffs and collar. A jeweled feather was pinned to the lapel, muted in the dull afternoon sky but likely sparkling in the sunlight. And really, did it matter? The blue in the stones matched the blue in her eyes, a detail he shouldn't have noticed but couldn't help focusing on.

And then he realized he was staring at her lapel, his gaze lingering in the general area of her ample bosom. If he were caught, it would result in a slap he well deserved.

Miss Poppy Featherstone.

She was as beautiful today as she was when he'd first met her a few years ago and as stunning as she'd been in London—when he'd been compelled to press his mouth to hers in a kiss that haunted him to this day.

A kiss that should never have happened. A step over lines he shouldn't have crossed. He'd known it before he'd done it and been incapable of stopping himself. The sweetest, most exquisite feeling. And he'd waited for the stinging slap after, but it hadn't been there. She'd stared at him in a way he'd never thought to see in a woman's gaze, never thought he'd deserve. Desire. Acceptance. Possessiveness. And it scared the hell out of him.

Scared him so much that he'd jumped at the news that he was needed back in Scotland. Not that he was pleased with the reason for his attendance either.

And now, here she was, sitting across from him. Every bone in his body wanted to lean forward and pull her into his embrace.

But there was something different about her now. A marked change he couldn't describe except to say the brilliant light he'd seen in her eyes when they'd danced in London last year was dimmed. Poppy had been witty, jovial, and charming. She was still charming, the wittiness still evidently there, but her jovial nature, the carefreeness of her disposition seemed... fragmented. The wind had been knocked out of her lively sails, and he wished more than anything to bring it back. There were fissures in the melancholy she'd wrapped herself in, and he continued to needle the cracks in hopes of opening her up while mending the merriness of her countenance.

Why he was so invested in her happiness was a mystery he didn't care to solve.

But he did think his sister's treatment of the three Featherstone women to be unkind. When he'd learned of Lord Cullen's passing and the entail not being passed to his daughters, Dougal had been surprised and then dismayed to learn they were having to rely on his sister's charity. Their half-brother Edward was a crack at billiards and a good man to hunt with, but when it came to his family, he bowed to Mary as if all the backbone he held at the club turned to ash as soon as he crossed his own threshold.

Dougal had always held hope that a good man would soften his sister. Edward was a good man—but he did nothing to soothe Mary's natural ire. Hell, even becoming a mother hadn't mollified her. If anything, it had only made her more annoyed at life. Dougal had come to the conclusion recently that there was literally nothing that could make Mary smile. She didn't even appear pleased when she hurt other people's feelings as most bullies did, having a sense of power and pleasure. Mary was just sour.

It wasn't charitable of Dougal to ponder his sister and her countenance in this way, but she'd been the same since they were children. She was bossy, selfish and prone to only caring about what other people might think in any given situation, then manipulating that situation to be in her favor and somehow still being mad about it.

Mary was forever a victim in all situations. Even if said situation was of her own making.

Of course, she'd agreed that the Featherstone lasses could live with her and Edward because not agreeing would make her out to be a bad person. Society would have looked down on her for being inhospitable and cold. Uncharitable. She couldn't have that. But that didn't mean she was going to make their time in her house pleasant. The opposite, Dougal guessed, so that they would leave on their own, and she could then prattle on about how she'd offered up her home and charity, and they'd not been grateful.

Which was quite sad, given that the Featherstone women were at their lowest. The loss of a parent had devastated his friends; even his own parents had been torn when they lost their mothers and fathers. He was lucky still to have his kicking up their heels, but that didn't mean he couldn't empathize. What the Featherstones needed was kindness and distraction. And he aimed to provide that if he could.

Dougal had felt the need to make up for his sister's behavior throughout their lives. This situation was no different.

As soon as he'd heard that the mourning women had moved in, he'd come down from his country estate in the Highlands to see if he might bring some cheer. Or, at the very least, act as a buffer between his sister and the Featherstones. Lord knew they were going to need it.

"We appreciate it. How long will you be in Edinburgh?" Miss Featherstone asked.

"A week or two," he drawled out, "Depending on the business I have to attend to."

"And what business is that?" She shifted, tucking the wool blanket closer to her waist. Her gaze was curious but hedging on unobtrusive from the way she explored the sidewalks next to their moving curricle.

"Family business." He didn't expect her to be interested in his business of horse flesh. Most women weren't. But he also didn't want to get into the fact that he wasn't actually in town on business.

"I see." She pursed her lips, and he sensed she was mildly offended by his lack of explanation.

Damn it. But it wasn't as if he could say he'd come there deliberately to see her.

"Well, I hope you're able to find success in your short time here, my lord. I used to help my father with his business, and it was satisfying. I know it's not really acceptable, but I've always had a good mind for maths, and Papa challenged me often with his ledgers."

Dougal chuckled. "If I ever find myself in a bind on the ledgers, I know who to ask for advice."

She glanced at him, a small smile on her lips. "You seem successful. I doubt you'll ever need my help."

"One never knows."

"That is true. One never does." At that, her face fell, and she quickly looked out the window again, and he realized he'd stepped in it, the conversation inadvertently touching on the quickness of her father's illness and death.

As they entered the park, a lone rider trotted beside them, a welcome distraction. "Ah, my good friend, Colonel Austen. Might I introduce you to Miss Poppy Featherstone and Miss Anise, the late Baron Cullen's daughters?"

Colonel Austen tipped his hat. "Ladies, you are the sun on this gloomy morning. And may I offer you my condolences on the loss of your father?"

"Thank you," Anise said, with a bat of her lashes and a subtle blush to her cheeks.

"We appreciate your thoughts," Poppy added, though she seemed far more subdued than her sister.

"Allow me to be of service should you need it," Colonel offered.

The two women nodded and practically whispered their thanks; their voices were so low. Dougal felt like his chest might split open.

Colonel Austen's gaze lingered on the down-turned face of Anise, an interest in his eyes that Dougal hadn't seen in years. Abruptly, he shook his head and turned his attention to Dougal. "How long are you in town?"

"A couple of weeks. Come by for dinner. I'll see that Mary adds a place for you at the table. Your company would be much appreciated."

Colonel Austen, who'd known Mary for as long as he'd known Dougal, given they were boyhood friends, chuckled. "I'd be delighted. How is tonight? I leave for the Highlands tomorrow morning."

Austen and Dougal had fought together in the military

and, prior to that, gone to Oxford together and Eton as lads. The only two Highlanders in their class, they'd had each other's backs during many a schoolyard fight. English aristocrats, having grown up believing the Scots were rubbish, had no problem pouncing on the two of them when their tutors weren't looking. And Dougal, as tough and well-built as he was, would have come away with a lot more bruises had it not been for his good friend helping him live to see another day.

"Then we'll be glad to have you with us before you head out of town." Dougal certainly would be, and he thought the Featherstones would be too. It meant that Mary would most likely be on her best behavior for the meal, which he wasn't certain had happened before his arrival.

"And you think that your sister will allow it?" Austen hedged. "There was that time last year that she practically dragged me out by my ear."

The two sisters looked up sharply, a smile on Poppy's lips.

"Of course, how could she deny a good friend a place at her table? And besides, we will no' be drunk before dinner this time."

Colonel Austen laughed. "We've been friends a long time, Mackay, and I've heard your sister deny many a name a place at her table—even when they were no' drunk."

Poppy bit back a laugh, and Dougal grinned. "My sister is a saint. I'll not hear another word of it." His tone dripped with sarcasm. "If anyone has been tossed out, it is certain that they deserved it."

"A saint, aye. I think ye refer to her husband," Austen drawled, which drew out a laugh from Anise.

"I assure you, our brother and his wife are well suited," Poppy said, surprising both himself and her sister, whose eyes widened.

But Colonel Austen only laughed. "Touché. Then I shall

come by early enough that she might invite me to stay for dinner herself, and we shall all swear to secrecy that this little plan was never hatched."

"And I will pray she does no' see through our schemes, for ye know how clever Mary is."

"And suspicious," Austen said.

"Always." Dougal nodded. "I was never able to get away with anything as a lad."

"Nor I."

"But ye were always so good to try and take the blame, though she never believed ye."

"Nay, Mary always believed punishments should be tilted in my direction."

"Indeed, she did."

"And still does. When I was here a few months ago, she made certain to give the servants the night off and lock up the house when I told her I was going to the club, and she asked me no' to."

"Locked out then?"

"Aye. And the sad thing is, I'd agreed to stay because she asked me to, even though I've got a house in town."

"Ye're a saintly brother. Perhaps tonight, we shall make a toast to the saints in our lives."

"I think it a good idea."

Poppy and Anise had perked up mightily now with the banter going back and forth. He hoped it would extend through the evening but had a feeling that when he returned to dinner, their joy might have been obliterated during tea, extinguished for life.

"It was a pleasure to meet the two of ye," Austen said, tipping his hat. "And I look forward to the delight of your company this evening."

"I don't know, Colonel Austen," Anise said, her voice a

touch cheeky. "I think I most look forward to the two of you riling up our sister-in-law."

"It's true. We will be happy to have her eagle gaze turned away from us for a moment." Poppy pressed her hands over her heart and let out an exaggerated sigh.

"A gift, to be sure," Anise added.

"We shall make it grand fun," Colonel Austen said.

"And perhaps we'll find all four of us turned out on our ears." Dougal imagined Mary dragging them all out and slamming the door in their faces. Sadly, it was an occurrence he'd witnessed before.

Poppy shrugged as if it were a foregone conclusion. "If that's the case, I've developed a good hand at cards, and Anise here has a talent for fortune-telling."

"Is that so?" Colonel Austen turned his interested gaze back on Anise.

She shrugged daintily. "Well, really, it's more like lucky guesses. But a number of things have come true. For example, our friend Rebecca did indeed get engaged last season and is expecting her first child."

"Don't forget the fortune you made about our cousin's wife."

"Oh, yes, I guessed that she would have to take care of her own wicked children, and seeing as how we left before she could hire anyone, that was also a fortune correctly told for at least a day or two."

"Indeed, it seems ye do have a talent for fortune-telling. Do tell me mine?" Colonel Austen said, leaning forward over his horse.

"I foresee a brandy before dinner and that you make it through dessert before Mary snaps that it's time for you to leave."

Colonel Austen chuckled. "I look forward to seeing your

fortune come to fruition, Miss Anise. Should we all get turned out, it sounds as if the two of ye might be able to survive out in the wild."

"Only time will tell," Poppy teased.

Dougal couldn't help but smile. With his friend's help, he had indeed accomplished his aim to distract the ladies from their grief and make them smile.

3

Though it didn't normally require much thought, breathing seemed to be a thing Poppy's body wasn't doing naturally anymore. And to make matters worse, while she concentrated on trying to take a breath, her knees felt unnaturally hot, as though the heat of Dougal's body was leeching the mere inch of space between them to taunt her flesh.

Despite the cool air brushing against her cheeks, her face felt hot, and she found herself looking anywhere but at him, now completely aware that he was having such an effect on her. In more ways than one. Of course, there was the physical, but beyond that, her mind was buzzing in a thousand different directions as though someone had unscrewed the top of her head and dumped an entire bee farm inside her brain.

Why was he being so nice?

Nice was good. It was great, fantastic even, but... He'd abruptly left her in London without a word. Why now? Why bother?

Glaringly evident was the fact that Dougal Mackay was

acting more concerned for their well-being than their own brother. That stung. She and Edward had used to be close. Before Mary. After Mary, there was a sudden change. No more popover visits. No more letters full of jests. No shopping trips and whirlwind journeys to London to take in the theatre.

But despite the distance that had ebbed between them over the last eight years or so, shouldn't he care a little bit? Though she supposed Edward thought he was doing a good deed by providing them with a roof over their heads, which to his credit, meant they weren't homeless, and that was important. And knowing Mary and her resistance, he'd had to put his foot down to get them even that much.

Also, hadn't it been her father who'd told her once never to expect more from someone than they'd proven willing to give? Edward had changed. And if the last eight years were any indication, she should stop expecting more. Stop expecting the brother she had once known to come back to her.

And if Edward and Mary didn't care about them, why did Dougal? She couldn't help but think that Dougal was up to something. Popping up so fortuitously now... What was his ulterior motive?

Try as she might, Poppy couldn't think of any reasons why a handsome, charismatic Scotsman would come down from his estate in the Highlands to parade her and her sister around town. Protect them, distract them from the machinations of Mary. And was it a coincidence that his friend happened upon them, and that said friend was coming to dinner, and that Anise was blushing ten shades of crimson every time Colonel Austen looked at her?

Poppy's mind was a whirl of questions and skepticism.

She rather hated that—and the pucker it surely gave to her face.

Skepticism was a new personality flaw that had popped up near the end of her father's life, and rather than abate with time as sorrow often does, it had only grown.

There had been little contingencies made for his daughters. A meager one hundred pounds a year, which was hardly enough for one person, let alone three, unless they were to move to the country and live in a small cottage, working the land themselves. A thousand pounds set aside for Anise and Poppy upon marriage was better than the per annum stipend, but there were plenty of other ladies in society who had more. And if Poppy were to be honest with herself and with Anise, most marriages were made based on alliances and money. That meant Poppy and Anise would be at the bottom of the proverbial barrel.

No other provisions had been made. As if her father hadn't planned to die or didn't care enough to see that his family was cared for in the afterlife. A hasty letter to his stepson—in addition to her mother's letter to Edward—pleading to provide housing had been the last of his attempts to see them not flung into the gutter for the rest of their lives.

There was no question that she and Anise needed to find suitable husbands—and quickly, or else they would be cut off without a penny. Or at least that is what their mother feared. Because Edward and Mary weren't going to let them live there indefinitely. Maybe not even to the end of the week.

Though she was Edward's mother, Lady Cullen had never been well-loved by her son, who seemed to have resented her marrying so quickly after his own father's death. But now, seeing the situation they were in, Poppy could understand it, even if Edward didn't realize that Baron Cullen had provided a roof over his young head.

Mother was even less loved by Mary, who somehow managed to conjure enough of a heart to smile at her son, though it often looked brittle enough to shatter.

One of their mother's greatest fears was that she would be left destitute, so she begged her daughters to marry as soon as possible so she might know at least she'd be kept well by one of them.

Poppy had just celebrated her twenty-first birthday, and Anise was barely over nineteen. Her sister had missed her coming out season due to their father's illness. And their mother, rightly so, had not thought it appropriate for Anise to be galivanting about town when their father was ill.

Of course, now Mother didn't feel she could ask Edward to give Anise the coming out she deserved.

And so, her sister was, in turn, quite unhappy not only at their father's passing but at what seemed to be the passing of her youth and place in society. No longer did she have much chance of a marriage match to a man of means—one who lived in the city and traveled to London. Anise had admitted late into the night that she feared she would be doomed to marry a countryman, one who didn't even own an evening jacket.

Poppy was lucky to have had a coming out season not only in Edinburgh but also in London last year. The season of the fated kiss. She'd seen plenty of opportunities with handsome men, but had squandered all her attention on the one man who'd abandoned her.

She stared now across the curricle at Dougal, who was grinning in jest at something Colonel Austen had said, which Poppy had completely missed.

Not paying attention to some of the other less charming

prospects was foolish now, in hindsight—and not at all like the sensible person she thought herself to be. But she'd not known her father was going to pass so quickly, and her heart had been claimed by a ruse. Nor did she know that they'd be at the mercy of her brother and his wife, whom she hadn't realized would grow more awful with each passing day. And most especially, she'd not known that Dougal was going to run away. That his kiss hadn't meant anything. The touch of their lips had been as fleeting as his last meal, it appeared.

If she'd had a crystal ball and knew the path of her future, she would have surely turned her back on him before it was too late, and they wouldn't find themselves in the current situation.

But she supposed she had the man sitting across from her to blame for that. Poppy frowned, leaning into her censure.

Dougal Mackay had been first introduced to her about five years prior when she was merely sixteen. And she thought it might have been love at first sight if such a thing existed.

He'd been dressed impeccably in a suit at her brother's wedding. And the moment he'd bent over her hand to kiss her palm, she'd practically swooned. He'd offered her one dance, and the feel of his hand on hers, the touch of his fingers at her waist, had her losing her breath faster than a too-tight corset.

The rest of the wedding ball, she'd wished for him to ask her to dance again, but he had not. Devastating really to a young lass like her, mooning over her first real crush. Of course, looking back now, she was a little embarrassed to have wished for a second dance. After all, he'd been twenty-two at the time, not interested in a fresh-faced adolescent girl who'd yet to come out in society. The only reason she was even allowed at the wedding ball was because the groom was her brother.

Otherwise, she would have been tucked up on the nursery with the rest of the children. Even Anise had been allowed one short dance, though she'd been fourteen. Anise's dance partner had been in uniform, not the colonel who rode beside them now, but another dashing hero. Anise had followed him around like a puppy until their mother sent them both upstairs for bed.

Then last year, when Poppy had come face-to-face with Dougal at the ball in London, she'd been shocked to see him. And shocked even more so by how her body reacted to being in his vicinity. All heartbeats and sweaty palms. Even her knees had knocked together a little bit, and she needed to get air.

Time had only made him more handsome. And apparently, it had only made her interest in him grow from a spark to a sizzling flame that ended in that devastating kiss.

But he'd expressed about as much interest in her last year as he had when she was sixteen—except his lips had roved from kissing the back of her hand to her mouth. Surely a hint that he'd loved her. And what now?

Oh, Poppy, you were so naïve.

"Are ye hungry?" Dougal's question jarred her, and Poppy worked to unwrinkle the frown on her forehead, the pinch of her lips, until she hoped she resembled someone more...or less.

Poppy shook her head, though really, she could eat. All the time. Her appetite was ravenous, likely given how active she was, pacing constantly, dancing when no one was looking and riding when she could. But her mother had warned her early and often that ladies—proper ladies—didn't have appetites and that she needed to rein in her desire for sustenance.

"What are you offering?" Anise asked, earning her an elbow from Poppy. "Ouch," she muttered.

"There's a delicious creamery just ahead. I thought the two of ye might like some iced cream."

Poppy's stomach growled in acceptance, and she hoped that no one heard it.

"Ah, do let me join ye," the colonel said jovially. "Their iced creams are to die for."

"I'd love to try one. Poppy?" Anise asked.

As much as she wanted to say no to keep up the appearance of being a lady, she also wanted to try it.

Relenting, Poppy said, "All right, but just a small bite."

"Ye're going to want more than a small bite after one taste," Dougal said.

"Indeed," the colonel agreed.

Poppy bit her tongue because his words resonated more deeply than for just a bowl of iced cream. One taste of his lips, and she'd been ready to sign over her life to him. Oh, what a scourge that kiss had been.

The carriage pulled to the side, and Dougal hopped down first, offering his hand to Poppy while the colonel waited to assist Anise.

"Feeling better?" Dougal leaned toward her, asking the question as if it were in confidence.

She hated how close they were. How the look in his eyes appeared so genuine. How her gaze accidentally moved to the corner of his mouth, where his lips curved into a smile that would surely melt all the creams inside.

Poppy shifted her gaze to the door of the creamery, cleared her throat, and hoped she sounded less than intrigued. "Yes, thank you."

Dougal didn't notice that she'd stiffened, his voice a caress as he said, "My pleasure."

Cad.

Why should it be his pleasure? By God, was he taunting her on purpose? Wanting her to fall in love with him all over again? Well, she refused. There was no time for her to be toyed with by Dougal Mackay all over again. Not when she needed to find a husband to save her mother from destitution and save her sister from making a mistake in an early marriage she wasn't ready for.

The inside of the creamery smelled like sugar and vanilla and chocolate decadence. Small round marble tables were in the shop with wrought iron chairs, mostly filled by ladies and gentlemen enjoying bowls of iced cream. Poppy's mouth watered, and she was fairly certain she was going to want to come back here and that she was going to eat more than one bite.

"What flavor would ye like?" Dougal asked.

"Strawberry," Anise said.

"My favorite. Good choice," the colonel replied.

"And ye, Miss Featherstone, what do ye think will be your favorite?"

Poppy glanced to the side where he was staring at her intently. Her favorite... Oh, but he was toying with her again. She sniffed and turned away, taking little pleasure in turning her nose up at him, even though she wished she could bathe in satisfaction at giving him the cut direct. "I think chocolate."

"An excellent choice."

She wanted him to hate her choice, not find it excellent.

Dougal and Colonel Austen retrieved the iced cream, bringing it to one of the small tables that Poppy and Anise had procured. Delicate scoops of light brown iced cream melted in her bowl. The first bite was heaven. The second felt like a decadent sin.

What a tease, bringing them to a place like this. She was going to be ruined forever.

It was hard for Poppy to eat each bite slowly without groaning in exquisite pleasure. After her third bite, she looked up to see Dougal watching her, his iced cream forgotten, and the look in his eyes akin to...desire.

Blast him!

Her face heated as he watched her, and she was suddenly self-conscious in a way she'd forgotten. Self-conscious in the way a man looks at a woman when he wishes to kiss her—a look she remembered quite well on him. Even then, she'd recognized it for what it was. That was something she'd seen when she was attending balls on the regular. But most of the men she'd been acquainted with—until Dougal had waltzed into London—were sticks-in-the-mud. And over the last year, none had compared, nor shown as much interest.

Dougal was no stick-in-the-mud but an exciting, intelligent, jovial man. The air in the room changed when he was there. His very presence could elicit a smile from even the sourest matron—except for Mary. No one could make Mary smile.

And perhaps that is why she'd been in love with him for the last five years. Because he lit up the world.

Well, perhaps *love* was a bit of a strong word. A more appropriate description might be that she, too, desired to kiss him every day for the rest of her life.

"Do you not like your iced cream?" she asked, staring at his melting bowl of chocolate hoping to get him to stop staring at her.

"I think I like yours better," he said.

Poppy almost choked, her spoon clicking against her teeth.

Colonel Austen tried to cover his laugh with a cough, accidentally inhaled his iced cream, and then coughed for real with Anise slamming her hand against his back.

"My goodness, Colonel, are ye well?" The question came from a young gentleman who'd entered the creamery along with a friend.

"Aye, Sir John, just fine."

Sir John's gaze moved to Anise, sitting beside Colonel Austen. "My lady, allow me to introduce myself. Sir John Ross at your service."

The young man was handsome—Poppy would give him that. A riot of brown curls and eyes that were the color of her iced cream. Tall, well-formed and impeccably dressed. The twinkle in his eye suggested he might also be a fun conversationalist, but there was something else there, just hidden beneath the surface, that gave Poppy pause. On instinct, she wasn't sure he was a man who could be trusted.

And from the way the colonel stiffened, she wondered if she was right.

"Mackay," Sir John said in greeting to Dougal.

"Sir John. What brings ye to Edinburgh?" Dougal, too, seemed to stiffen in the young man's presence.

"Business, and ye?"

"Aye, same." Dougal glanced at Poppy, and she wished she could read what was going on behind those eyes. "Sir John and I are practically neighbors, as is Colonel Austen here."

"Ah." She nodded as if she understood but truly was as confused as she'd been before, and her chocolate was melting into a puddle.

"Would you care to join us?" Anise suggested, to which Colonel Austen, Poppy and Dougal stared at her in shock.

Anise was batting her lashes prettily, and Poppy wanted to groan.

"A grand invitation, but I'm afraid I canna stay. Perhaps I could call on ye tomorrow at..." he asked.

"Of course. We're staying with my brother, Lord Leven."

"Until then." Sir John bowed slightly and then left the creamery, apparently having only entered upon seeing Colonel Austen and Dougal.

Was it Poppy's imagination, or had she picked up on some sort of rivalry?

Poppy wanted to yank Anise by the arm to somewhere private where she could ask what had gotten into her flirting with Sir John and encouraging him, but that would only draw attention to them both, which she didn't want to do. And besides, she also could understand her sister's motivation to act that way. They were, after all, both in need of a husband. Perhaps she should let her sister know she was willing to take on the responsibility of marrying a man she didn't love so that Anise could fall in love.

The conversation from that point was dampened. The colonel looked deep in thought, and Dougal tried to pick up the cheer, but nothing worked. Sir John, it appeared, had waltzed into the creamery and dumped saltwater on all their sweets.

They left the creamery and climbed back into the carriage.

"I bid ye adieu," Colonel Austen said, tipping his hat. "A pleasure meeting ye both. I shall see ye at dinner."

"You are welcome any time. We look forward to your continued company," Anise said, shocking Poppy.

Was Anise angling for both Colonel Austen and young Sir John? What game was she playing?

"A pleasure indeed, Miss Anise." He took Anise's hand

and pressed a kiss to the air above her glove and then did the same to Poppy.

For Poppy, their return curricle ride to the house was filled with trepidation. Flashes of Mary's snarls, Mother's sad sighs, Edward's frowns. Besides, despite the ride and the stop for iced cream, it was not nearly time yet for tea. Which meant Poppy would either need to hide in her room or deal with Mary in the drawing room. The latter of which sounded tantamount to torture.

Isolation seemed a better bet. And at least she shared a room with Anise and could ask her just what she was thinking with encouraging both men, and that it wasn't necessary for her to do so.

Dougal helped the two of them down from the carriage, and as they walked up the path to the door, held open by the butler, he said, "I thank ye both for taking the time to accompany me. It's always rather awkward when I go and get an iced cream by myself."

"It was lovely, thank you," Anise said, and then she hurried inside and up the stairs, leaving Poppy alone to bid Dougal farewell.

Poppy's smile was tight as she tried to keep her emotions inside. "It was a pleasure, my lord. And I think I've found a new indulgence I'll have to avoid." *You being the first.*

"I think if ye find something ye love, why not indulge?" Though he was speaking of iced cream, she couldn't help but think of their past together. And how much his words could have represented that moment.

She decided to answer directly regarding the sweets. "My dresses would not agree."

Dougal chuckled. "Nothing an extra walk or ride willna accommodate."

"Perhaps you're right." But she still wasn't going to do it.

Especially knowing he frequented the venue. Running into him unnecessarily would only hurt her more.

He winked. "Perhaps."

Oh, why did he have to wink at her? The teasing, taunting deliciousness of it was too much. Her smile faltered, and she turned away from him, needing the sanctity of her room and the door that would separate her from him. As she climbed the stairs from somewhere, Mary's shrill voice could be heard admonishing someone. Poppy doubted it was her son, as the sweet four-year-old could do no wrong. Likely a servant or even Edward, as Mary seemed to be the queen of this castle.

"Goodbye for now," Dougal called after her.

"We shall see you at tea?" Poppy asked, glancing over her shoulder and remembering too late that Mary had said no.

"I will try to sneak in, but my sister is verra particular about who attends, and I'm no' usually on the list." His laughter traveled up the stairs to stroke her skin.

"A shame. I think you may have been the most interesting guest." She shrugged, emboldened by the distance the stairs put between them to tease him back.

He grinned, and even with the length of distance between them, she saw it for how handsome it was. "I'm certainly no', but I shall see ye at dinner."

"Are you staying here?" The question was perhaps inappropriate, but she was curious just how much she would have to avoid him.

"I have a house just down the row."

Thank goodness. "That is very convenient to be so close to your sister when you're in town."

Dougal raised a brow. "I'm no' certain I would call it convenient. Maybe something a little more akin to problematic."

"How so?" Poppy couldn't help asking, even though now that she'd reached the top stair, she really should run away.

Mary's voice was growing closer, and the two of them glanced around, trying to locate which direction she was coming from. The way her voice echoed it was as if she were descending from the ceiling itself.

"I find being close to my sister to be a little...distracting," was all he said. "Though, with the ladies Featherstones as her guests, it is less so."

"Well, I do hope not distraction enough to keep you from your business."

"No' at all."

"Dougal." Mary's voice was sharp as appeared before them rather suddenly as if she'd seeped from the walls. "My tea will be starting soon."

"Is that an invitation?"

Poppy pressed her lips together to keep from laughing, for Mary's declaration had such a sharp edge that she might have sliced him to ribbons with the insinuation that he should leave immediately. Slowly, she backed away from the stairs, hoping she wouldn't be seen.

"You know it's not," she practically bit out. "But you may come to dinner."

"I accept."

Mary stared at him. There seemed to be more she wanted to say, but she managed to keep herself in line.

"Miss Featherstone," Dougal waved to where Poppy stood, and Mary flashed a shocked, then irritated, look.

Poppy held in the sigh that begged to be let out, forced herself not to crack, and waved to Dougal.

"Until this evening, then," he said, backing out of the house, a mischievous grin on his too-handsome face.

"Well," Mary called up the stairs after he'd left. "Don't set your designs on my brother. You'll only be disappointed."

Poppy eyed her sister-in-law. "Designs?"

"I can see what's happening here. And I won't allow it."

Poppy bit her tongue to keep herself from retorting something unkind. As if Mary would have any say in Poppy's future. Her dowry had been written into their father's will for Edward to execute—much to the chagrin of her Cousin Thomas who wished to control everything—and there was no way that her brother would go against what their father wanted. Besides, she'd gone for a carriage ride and a sweet treat—that did not make a marriage proposal.

And she was pretty certain Mary did not know about the kiss from last year that Dougal deemed unimportant.

"I'm not certain what you mean," Poppy said innocently. "I should go prepare for tea."

Though her back was to Mary as she retreated to her room, she could feel her sister-in-law's eyes burning into her skull.

❦ 4 ❧

Dougal crumpled the letter his aunt had sent him and tossed it in the fire, watching the edges turn black until the entire thing was one orange flame and then gray, smoldering ash.

The reminder from his elderly relation that if he wanted to receive the rest of his inheritance, he had to wed was a reminder he didn't need. Nor did he need or want the reminder that a decade ago, he'd made a declaration to a young lady whom he hadn't seen or heard from in years. To think that she'd decided now, of all times, to pick up a pen and whisk off a note to his aunt. The nerve...the oddity of it all.

Vows from men not yet twenty shouldn't be taken seriously, nor should they be followed up on, and yet that was exactly what his aunt was insinuating. Lucia Steventon was a name he'd rather forget. The folly of youth was really what her name brought to mind. On his nineteenth birthday, he'd met a girl at a house party in Edinburgh. By the end of the night, after one too many drinks, he'd declared that if by his twenty-ninth birthday he was not married, he would marry her.

He poured himself a finger of whisky, thought better of it and made it two, then swallowed it, attempting to quell some irritation, but the drink did not do the trick.

Why on earth would Lucia have taken him seriously?

And why on earth would his aunt recall his letter from ten years ago in which he'd told her all about it? Surely, she would have burned the memory from her mind as he'd burned her reminder.

As if this upcoming twenty-ninth birthday of his would make a difference in his life or his declarations. Aye, he'd like to receive the rest of his inheritance, but not at the price it would cost—marrying Lucia Steventon, who was practically a stranger to him at this point. He wasn't even certain that he would recognize her if he passed her on the street.

Since his drunken declaration, they'd had a few letters passed between the two of them. Danced at a few balls and happened upon each other at a house party or two, but it had been years since he'd seen her, and on none of those occasions had she attempted to solidify the childish attachment.

The idea of marrying her made his mood darken. Hell, the fact that his aunt was demanding he surrender his bachelorhood was what irked him even more, for she was usually entirely rational.

Lucia Steventon had been nice, stoic, and pleasant enough to look at but boring. Not challenging at all, and not a great conversationalist either, from what he could recall. The reason he'd fallen for her was lost on him now.

The idea of marrying her made him cross, but it also brought visions of another woman to the forefront of his mind.

A woman he didn't want to disappoint by telling her that

he'd made the stupid mistake of practically proposing marriage to a stranger when he was an adolescent. That when he'd kissed her on the terrace at the ball in London and had seen how she looked at him, the feelings that look had given him... Oh, for feck's sake. He was a coward. That was the real reason he'd left London. Afraid of what it would mean to be a man Poppy Featherstone would depend on.

Afraid to fail her.

Afraid his past would come tunneling up the moment the engagement was printed in the newspaper.

Because even though he'd chalked up his declaration to Lucia as nothing more than boyhood idiocy, it would appear from the current situation, she had clearly not. And because he was a gentleman—and a fecking coward—he'd never had the heart to bring it up to her in the last decade. Which he clearly should have. But ten years was a long time. He'd assumed he'd be married by then—assumed she would have been too. And he would be off on some other adventure with Lucia Steventon nothing more than a fleeting memory.

After all, could they truly call that a proposal? A drunken nineteen-year-old down on one knee promising matrimony a decade from then? It was not a betrothal. Not a promise he was old enough to have made in the first place. Nor sober enough, for that matter.

Dougal sat at his writing desk and penned a note to his aunt saying just that. He was not beholden to a promise made ten years prior when he was barely a man. At the time Lucia had barely been old enough to accept. Had she truly been pining for him all this time? That would make her nearly his own age. What woman in her right mind would wait so long to get married? Men of society considered women past their twenty-second year to be practically expired when it came to child-bearing—a fact he knew was ridiculous considering his mother had been in her thirties when she'd birthed him. But still, why would Lucia risk missing her child-bearing ticking clock?

Guilt ebbed into his chest to think the silly chit had been waiting for him for a decade.

And also, incredulity. If she'd been truly anticipating a knock at her door, a ring presented in earnest, all this time, then why had she waited until now to inform his aunt of the promise? For that matter, why had she contacted his aunt and not him?

Or was this some trick of his aunt's? Very unlike her to do such a thing.

He thought of Mary. How, when he'd arrived in Edinburgh a few days ago, she'd glowered. Was this her way of getting rid of him? Now, he could see being meddlesome. And she certainly didn't like the idea of him hanging around the Featherstone lasses. But as far as he knew, the idiotic declaration he'd made a decade ago was unknown to Mary. Unless his aunt had told her. Or Lucia herself. So many questions converged in his mind, and none of them came with an answer. Just an endless swirl of self-reproach and a mess getting messier the more he thought about it.

Coming to Edinburgh to help the Featherstone lasses had put another complication into his stratosphere. Poppy.

The moment he'd seen her—the shock that had registered on her face. Then, the resentment was swiftly replaced by softness, only to be filled with hurt a moment later. Those expressions had continued throughout their ride in the park and even as they ate their iced creams.

The resentment and hurt he deserved. The softness—which showed she still might have feelings for him—he did not.

Poppy still fascinated him. From the moment he'd first

laid eyes on her, he'd fallen for the tease in her eyes and the quirk to her mouth that made him want to spend hours with her. To dig deeper and find out just what made her tick.

And she'd returned his interest until he'd mucked it all up.

Now this. If there'd been any chance of him trying to salvage what they'd started a year ago, Lucia Steventon was here to ruin it. Hell, he was the one ruining it. Lucia just happened to be the catalyst to move his downfall along.

"Blast it," he growled, sealing the envelope to his aunt. He marched out of his library and handed the letter to his butler. "See that this is delivered to my aunt right away."

"Aye, my lord."

Dougal trudged upstairs to his bedchamber, needing to dress for dinner.

He cursed the entire time, imagining every scenario, including one where Lucia happened to be at dinner. Lord help him, he'd leave.

But leaving would mean he lost any chance of being in Poppy's company again. She might be willing to forgive him for the way he'd departed the year before, but there was no way that he could even expect to be allowed in her presence if he disappeared again.

All he could hope for was that today would be the last day he ever heard the name Lucia Steventon. Though he had a feeling the past was coming back to bite him hard on the arse, and there was no way he was going to get away without a chunk of himself missing.

$\underset{\sim}{\text{s}}$ 5 $\underset{\sim}{\text{s}}$

A s fast as she scurried toward her room, Poppy was surprised she hadn't lit the carpet runner on fire. She checked to make sure, prepared to see smoke rising from the wool pile, but the Leven green, blue and white tartan remained unscathed.

As she stared down the hallway, Poppy wrenched open the door, half expecting Mary to chase after her, but only the ghost of Mary's ire followed. She closed the door quickly behind her, clicking the lock into place just in case, which caused Anise, who was scribbling furiously in her diary, to drop her quill and look up at her worriedly.

"Mary," Poppy said as if that were enough explanation.

Anise nodded and went back to dashing off her sentences.

One day, might they say things like, "Oh, I was just Mary'd." Or "My goodness, don't be such a Mary." Sad really, how one bad Mary's attitude put such a stigma onto another. She knew plenty of Marys who were nothing but sweet.

"What's got you so frenzied?" Poppy asked.

Anise dropped her pen again to flop back in her chair and

dramatically press her hands over her heart. "Oh, Sir John, wasn't he a dream?"

Poppy shrugged, frowning a little. Dream was really an exaggeration, wasn't it? "Hard to say, as we were only acquainted with him for a few minutes. I thought the colonel rather charming."

Anise rolled her eyes.

Poppy crossed the room to take up the chair by the window. "Why are you rolling your eyes?"

"He's boring." Anise made the word "boring" sound utterly dull, the way she dragged it out and added a nasal twinge to it.

Poppy didn't agree. Colonel Austen seemed to have more personality than Sir John in the few minutes they'd gotten to know him, but perhaps she could be persuaded otherwise. She was coming to things from a practical standpoint. Anise, more often than not, went about her judgments from the heart. Both methods had their merits and, when put together, could be very complimentary of one another. If one wasn't so stubborn—that was the hurdle most days.

"I think you find Sir John more interesting because he was a little closer to your age," Poppy suggested.

"And yours. The colonel had to be thirty at least. Practically ancient. Do you think Sir John is attached?"

Poppy bit the inside of her cheek. Thirty wasn't ancient at all. In less than ten years, she would be thirty, and she hardly considered those meager number of years would make her suddenly decrepit. But she supposed that it might seem aged for Anise, who was not yet even twenty. Poppy kicked off her slippers and tucked her feet up under her legs. "Couldn't say, but I doubt he would have volunteered to come and call on you if he was. That would be an insult to his fiancée."

"Good point." Anise rested her chin on her hand and

stared into space, her eyes mooning over some imagined romance. Poppy could practically see the affair playing out before her, and if Anise kept looking off like that, she was liable to end up rushing off with Sir John before she knew him properly enough to ascertain if he had a middle name.

"You know," Poppy hedged, "it's not your responsibility to marry yet. No need to settle for just anyone."

The glazed look in Anise's eyes faded, and she focused on her sister with a frown but didn't say anything, which was rather unlike her. Her silence was worrisome.

"What is it?" Poppy urged, one stockinged foot unfolding to press to the floor as if that might somehow ground her.

"Mama has made it clear one of us should marry soon to secure our future."

"And that responsibility should fall to me as the eldest sister," Poppy said. "You should wait until you're in love."

Anise's frown increased, adding a hint of not quite malice but something akin to it. "And yet you've had all this time and not seen to it." She flung her hand toward the door. "Locking us in here because our sister-by-marriage is a tyrant. This is no way to live."

Perhaps another sister would take offense to Anise's tirade, but not Poppy. She was used to her sister blaming her for things, even if they weren't her fault. And there was a measure of truth in what Anise said. Poppy had not tried hard enough to entice any bachelors into asking for her hand. But she'd been mending a foolishly broken heart. She wasn't at all surprised at Anise's thoughts put to words. After all, she knew her sister well, and she knew herself just as much. They were close friends most of the time, but every once in a while, Anise, being the younger sister by two years, would feel a sense of competition, the need to prove herself. And in this instance, she thought Poppy had done them a disservice and that she would step in to right it.

Poppy was mostly patient regarding her sister and let her antics go. But in this situation, she could not. Anise was only nineteen and, most of the time, acted quite a lot younger. She'd lived a sheltered life, not that Poppy too hadn't been coddled by their doting parents, but Anise especially had been.

In this situation, Poppy wasn't going to make it a competition. There was no argument; she would take care of them, and Anise would need to understand that. "There was not a sense of urgency previously," Poppy said, trying to compassionately relay that with Papa alive, she hadn't needed to marry so swiftly. "We couldn't have known that what has come to pass would be so soon."

Anise squared her shoulders, digging in her heels. "Perhaps we should have."

Poppy could see she was going to need to be a bit stronger with her sister than she wanted to be. Well, she wasn't unused to fighting with her. And this time, she wasn't going to back down.

"Perhaps we might have, but we didn't. And death is never something scheduled, is it, sister? Rather popping up when you least expect it or want it. And we cannot live our lives with a knife to our throat. Rushing into one decision after another without consideration because someone might die."

A knock sounded at the door, and their mother's sweet voice sounded on the other side as she jiggled the locked door. Anise bounced up and unlocked the door with a look toward Poppy that said, "See what you did," though she'd done nothing.

Mama walked in, her face rather pale, wringing her hands.

Anise, duty done by unlocking, returned to her seat at the writing desk.

"My dears, I think we have a bit of an issue." Mama looked ready to faint.

Poppy hurried over to her mother, taking her elbow and guiding her to their chaise longue to sit. "What is it?"

"I am not normally a sneak."

"Of course."

"But I overheard something I perhaps should not have."

"Tell us, Mama," Anise said, putting down her pen and twisting in her desk chair to face them.

Their mother glanced toward the door as if someone might burst through it, catching them in a bit of gossip.

"Mary was...well, she was speaking rather loudly, to be sure, and I happened to pass by the door, and I'd not have normally stopped, but I couldn't help myself."

Poppy bit her lip to keep from telling her mother to get on with the story already.

"She was telling Edward that since he's been put in charge of dispensing your dowries, he should figure a way to lower your dowries and think of their own son's legacy—keeping the rest for their child as payment for boarding us now. That a thousand pounds each was too much to give and that all the food and extra work for the servants now was somehow taking away from their child."

"But how? Edward didn't inherit Papa's money and properties. That all went to our cousin. He's only the executor of our dowries. It hardly seems legal."

"Exactly." Mama pulled a fan from her sleeve and started to air her face, drawing in her breaths quickly. "She is going to rob you girls in any way she can, no matter the law. And me. My first husband, Edward's father, left me a house in the Highlands. I've had it let out for years, the small amount of money going back to the land, but she even suggested he sell it. Sell my house."

Poppy had known about the country house. And the only reason they hadn't gone there instead of begging Edward's charity, was because moving to the country meant giving up any hope whatsoever of them finding suitable matches.

"Nay, Mama, Edward won't agree. He's not so mean. And besides, why would he risk it?"

Their mother shook her head. "When it comes to Mary, Edward doesn't seem to have a voice any longer. She also said..." Mother fanned herself harder. "That you weren't really his sisters, being that you were from another father, and there was no way to prove that I was really his mother since no witnesses to his birth were alive—except me."

To even suggest such a thing was mind-boggling. Poppy's mouth popped open repeatedly and then shut as she tried to wrap her head around what Mary was insinuating. "That absolute wench," Poppy said loud enough that it covered the expletive murmured by Anise—thank heavens or their mother would have fainted right away. "Is she claiming Edward was switched at birth? In that case, there's no way to prove that his father is his father. What a can of worms she's trying to open. And for what? We've never done anything to deserve her ill-treatment."

"I always thought her a bit of a viper, but I never thought she'd let her venom out. Nor did I think Edward would be poisoned so heartily. He was always such a strong-minded lad." Mama shook her head. "But I heard him say nothing to naysay her. And I mean nothing. She could have been talking to herself for all I know."

"Perhaps she was merely practicing her speech to convince him," Anise offered.

Mama shook her head. "I'm afraid the noise was coming

from his study. I doubt she would have been practicing alone there. Too many ways to get caught, though she'd talk her way out of it. She's quite bold, but I don't think that bold."

"I wouldn't put it past her," Anise said.

"Nor would I. I don't understand. Why does she loathe us so much?"

"Some people, Mary being one of them, are inexplainable," Mama said. "There doesn't seem to be a reason other than it is just who she is."

"I think you're right, Mama. Should I talk to Edward? Remind him of his duty and the illegalities of what she's suggesting? The trust will not just fall to him. It can't. And he can't take away your house."

"I had never wanted to put a voice to this, but I thought that house might be our saving grace if we cannot stay here."

Poppy hardly remembered the house in the Highlands, save for the one summer they'd gone to stay there. It was small, and felt quite rustic. They had pretended to be farmers those few weeks and had a lovely time. The memories of the cottage weren't so bad. But it wasn't a place she wanted to live. So remote...so far from any person, it would not be suitable for two young ladies in need of a husband.

Poppy and Edward had been close growing up. His father had passed when he was barely out of leading strings, and their mother, desperate not to find herself in the situation she now faced, had married quickly. Until he'd vowed his life to Mary, Poppy might have even said he was one of her best friends. But things changed after his marriage. And Edward started to look at her differently.

Started to treat all of them differently, including his own mother.

Even now, in this massive townhouse in Edinburgh with plenty of bedchambers, she and Anise were forced to share.

They'd not shared a room since they were in the nursery together. And it wasn't as if there weren't plenty of other rooms to be had. There were at least a dozen bedrooms in this house. She remembered running through them when they played seek-and-find as children.

This house had once belonged to Edward's father's father, passing to Edward when he was in his late adolescence.

But Mary had insisted that only two rooms be used for his mother and sisters. That only one maid be assigned between the three of them, though they had plenty of servants too.

"I think a conversation is a good idea," her mother said, her shoulders slightly straightening as she said it. "Any time I try to get close to Edward, Mary shows up and intervenes. Almost as if she has some magical insight to mine and Edward's proximity."

"She does the same with me," Poppy said, thinking of what had happened earlier in the foyer with Dougal. "But I'm willing to give it a try, all the same. It can't hurt us more than she already has."

"Perhaps I can distract her," Anise offered.

"A distraction is a good idea. Do it during tea, Poppy?" Mama suggested. "Feign a headache and excuse yourself. She won't be able to leave her guests to find you. And Anise, if she does try to follow Poppy, you should engage her somehow, perhaps with a question the other ladies might be interested in knowing. I'll add on to it for good measure to keep her from leaving."

"Good idea." Poppy hadn't wanted to go to tea anyway. The very idea of watching Mary parade around as if she were some sort of savior and they the lonely paupers who needed her charity was ridiculous. The entire situation was ludicrous and backwards, especially when Edward should rightfully be able to support his own mother. And more so, the dowries belonged to Poppy and Anise, and the house belonged to their mother. None of it was stamped with Mary's name, as much as she was attempting to wrestle it away.

With their plan in place, Mama and Anise went down to tea at the given time. Poppy decided not to go at all, fearing that Mary, in all her machinations, would be able to bar her from leaving.

Even in her room, Poppy could hear the chatter of feminine voices. She was curious what kind of gossip they might be getting up to, but she remained as planned for at least the first quarter-hour in case Mary did decide to check on her or send her maid up.

Poppy thought perhaps she might have gleaned a bit of her sister's pretend fortune-telling because approximately seven minutes after Poppy said she had a megrim and wouldn't be coming to tea, there was a knock at the door, and Mary's own maid came in with a tray of tea that smelled like an old lady's hat.

Poppy lay in bed, the curtains drawn, the lights doused, pretending she was struck hard with an ache in her head.

The maid wasn't there just to serve tea. She was also snooping, even going so far as to pretend to tuck her in to feel the temperature on her forehead. When she fussed about for another five minutes—including "tidying" Poppy's writing desk, perhaps looking for evidence of some sort—Poppy worried that she had been sent to make sure Poppy didn't leave her room, but the woman eventually did depart. And thankfully, it was thirty seconds before Poppy was going to demand she leave, which would have been even more suspicious.

Poppy waited another five minutes to be sure the woman wasn't going to come back, and then she crept to her bedroom door and pulled it open, peering out, afraid of being caught. Afraid of seeing the snooping maid standing sentry, or perhaps even Mary to say, "Ah-ha! I knew you were faking."

But the corridor was blessedly empty. Poppy slipped out of her room, shutting the door silently behind her. She remained still in case the maid popped out of some hidden place, but she was utterly alone.

At this time of day, her brother would either be in his study, or he would have sneaked off to his club—which, if it were the latter, she was out of luck. *Please be in your study; please be in your study...* She silently repeated the mantra the entire way.

Down the stairs she crept, terrified the whole time, heart pounding, afraid the nosey maid or one of the ladies would depart tea and see her, but she somehow made it outside her brother's study, knocked, and he called for her to enter.

She pulled open the door, stepped through and only breathed when it shut behind her.

"Poppy." He smiled, some of the tension in his features melting as he saw her.

And for just a moment, she remembered them as children playing chase. And the way he always tried to include her, even though his friends thought him odd for doing so.

"May I sit?" she asked, indicating the chair opposite him.

"Of course." He closed the ledger he'd been working in and focused on her, and she wondered if he thought it odd that she was there instead of attending the tea. But he didn't say anything to indicate that. Was it too much to hope that he still knew her well enough to understand she'd find a way out of having tea with Mary?

"What can I do for you?" he asked after she'd settled in the chair.

Poppy licked her lips, which felt suddenly dry, her fingers

clasped tightly in her lap. "I wanted to speak with you about my dowry. And about Mama's house."

Edward's features shuttered enough that it reinforced what their mother had thought she heard. Mary hadn't been practicing her tirade. Those demands had been very, very real.

"I wanted to speak with you as well," he said, all but confirming. "I think it best that you, Anise and your mother move to the dower house in the Highlands."

Poppy stilled. Her mind was suddenly obliterated of all thought, as if lightning had somehow come through the roof and into the study, jolting her brain. He wasn't going to sell Mama's house, but her other fear of isolation appeared to be coming true.

"At the end of the season?" she prompted, hoping that was the case. That Edward was going to give them a fighting chance.

Edward shook his head and wouldn't meet her eye, finding the items on his desk to be much more interesting. "Nay, I think now. As soon as possible."

"But Edward, why?"

"Mary thinks it best for everyone. It's time for Mother to go to the dower house my father left for her, and it would be best if you both accompanied her."

At least he wasn't denying that she was his mother, nor was he denying her what his father had left her. There was no mention of her and Anise's dowries either. Perhaps moving them out now was his way of saving them from his wife. And himself from any more of Mary's tantrums.

"How will we marry, Edward, being shut away from society?"

Her brother had the audacity to chuckle. "Certainly, there are men in Highlands. Do you think all those who live there were plopped from the sky?"

"We don't live in medieval times, and we aren't country people. We're not farmers or what have you. Ladies and gentlemen go to their country estates in the Highlands for house parties and hunting parties. We don't even know who they are. We'll be lucky to get an invitation. You are locking us in a closet."

"Oh, you are being dramatic, sister. The dower house is not as isolated as you think. And I'm certain there will be plenty of invitations." He finally looked at her, some warmth around the edges, but it was hard to pinpoint. "I want the both of you to marry, trust me. Besides, it's decided." Whatever warmth she thought she'd caught a glimpse of disappeared.

Poppy sat rigid, devastated. And when she wanted to collapse backward into the chair, to let the frustrated tears take over, the stubborn part of herself, the part that didn't want Edward to see he'd hurt her, kept her spine upright and the tears at bay.

When she'd walked into his study, with the way he'd smiled, she'd thought that he still felt some affection for her. But her mother was right. Mary had poisoned him against them, and he would now send them away to fade into nonexistence. And if they didn't marry, then what? Was that his end game, to outlive them and claim their dowries himself? It didn't work that way, but somehow, Mary had convinced him it would. And it was evident now that Edward was firmly within Mary's grasp.

The only good thing to come of this was that at least he wasn't taking the house, nor yet taking the dowries. He was defying Mary in two small ways. But still...he was banishing them from society, which still hurt.

"I beg you to reconsider, Edward. Anise is only nineteen. Surely, she would benefit from being in society."

"She could also do with some humility." Edward stood, glaring down at her as if he needed the leverage to make himself heard.

Gone were the affections of a brother she'd once loved so much.

Poppy stood. She was tall for a woman, and Edward was short. Their heights were equal when they were both on their feet, eye to eye. "Locking her up in the Highlands won't change her."

"I beg to differ." He slapped his desk, the veins in his next starting to pop as his cheeks reddened. "And please do stop saying I'm locking you up. You'll have a lovely house in the country, and the three of you will make good company for each other. I don't want to hear another word about it. As I said, it's decided. Now, you'd best get back to tea. It's highly improper for you to have left Mary's tea to find me."

She didn't bother to tell him that she'd never even entered the drawing room. "And it's highly improper for a brother to rob his sisters of a life." She stood up, angry now and not caring what she said. "You should be ashamed, Edward. It was your duty to protect us after our father passed."

He glared up at her. "I am protecting you."

And she could see in his eyes that he truly believed it.

Poppy was too stunned, too dismayed, to say another word.

But in her mind, at that moment, she determined she would never marry someone who might have the power to influence her thoughts, beliefs, and values. Edward, the brother she'd always admired, was no longer a person she wanted to be nor a person she could respect.

The dining room at Edward's house had air thicker than the clam chowder served at dinner.

Dougal looked from somber face to somber face—the Featherstone women, the pinched expression that made Mary look as if she had aspirations of becoming a prune. Edward's face was even worse. Looked as if the chap had taken a blow to the ballocks and was still feeling the residual ache.

Colonel Austen sat beside Dougal, the Featherstone ladies across the table from them, and Mary and Edward at their respective head positions. Dougal and Austen had attempted to make good conversation, but Mary seemed bent on either shutting them down or putting a firm damper on anything jovial. She was not pleased that Austen was attending dinner. And not because setting an extra place was hard or because there wasn't enough food. No, she was displeased because she was Mary, and Mary didn't like anything that wasn't her idea.

After his and Austen's initial starts to the conversation, Lady Cullen, too, had tried to engage them all with talks of an opera playing at Covent Garden, but Mary's snipe was so shrill as to practically crack the wine glass she was holding. Subsequently, not a word was uttered.

The clink of silverware on china echoed melancholily in the vast room. Even the footmen, who stood ready with drinks and dishes to be served, looked uncomfortable in the strange atmosphere. One poor chap nearly spilled the chowder on Mary when she made an aggressive hand gesture toward Austen at his talk of a horse race he'd been to last week.

If only Dougal could somehow record Mary's antics for her to see. Surely, she wouldn't want to be depicted in the light in which she currently cast herself. An artist's rendering might show her as a great, snarling beast. A demon who had come crawling from the earth.

Dougal took a sip of his wine and cleared his throat, needing to break the silence, no matter how painful his sister's retaliation was. "The chowder is superb."

Mary swiveled her head in his direction, her pinched visage looking almost surprised now to see him sitting there. What world had she been living in? He wondered, and would even pay money, to see what things went on in his sister's head. If only to better figure out how to behave around her.

"Of course it is. We would only have the best cooking, using the best ingredients."

"A delight to know ye are so lucky." He tried smiling, but Mary bared her teeth at him and then set her spoon down, signaling for the footman to take her bowl, which was probably a good idea, before she threw it at Dougal.

"How was tea?" Dougal tried again in hopes of parting the gloom.

Mary opened her mouth to speak, but Edward's voice cut across the table. "I'm going to my club. Mackay, Colonel Austen, care to join me?"

Dougal practically choked on his tongue. Edward would cut off Mary? That was a new development...

"But we've only been served the first course," Mary said, her figure held so tightly Dougal was worried she might shatter.

"I've not got an appetite, my dear." Edward pushed back his chair, making it clear he had no interest whatsoever in arguing with her and would not have his mind changed.

How shocking.

And as much as he would have loved to escape his sister and enjoy an evening on the town, the last thing that Dougal wanted to do was leave the dining room to go to the club with Edward. They'd never been friends, and considering the three Featherstone women looked as if someone had kicked their puppies, he would much rather get to the bottom of that situation. He did not want to leave them tonight and know they would be unhappy, and at the mercy of Mary's poor temper.

However, Edward stared at him in a way that said he wasn't welcome to stay in his home, and Dougal could practically hear his sister seething. If he dared to look at her, he might see that her steaming ears were causing the wallpaper to bubble. Not wanting to create a scene he might not be able to come back from, he, too, pushed back his chair and stood.

Colonel Austen placed his folded napkin on the table and rose, his eyes on the youngest Featherstone, mirroring the same regret Dougal felt at being dismissed. The way Poppy was staring at him now practically shouted, "Traitor!"

And saints, did he feel that. Alas, there was naught he could do about it. There was always tomorrow; he'd come and call and find out what was going on unless he could needle it out of Edward tonight.

Dougal bowed to the ladies present. "Until we meet again, I bid ye all a good night."

"Thank you, Lord Reay," the Lady Cullen said softly.

Anise smiled weakly, out of character for the normally vibrant lass.

But most disturbing was the coldness in Poppy's eyes as she met his. "Goodnight, my lord."

And then she returned her attention to her chowder, which, though she'd spooned plenty, had yet to be eaten. She swirled the creamy base but did not take a bite.

"Lady Cullen, Miss Featherstone, Miss Anise, I have truly enjoyed making your acquaintance." Colonel Austen bowed, regret etched in the corners of his mouth.

More guilt added to Dougal's shoulders. He knew his friend had been eager to join them and was obviously interested in Anise, which perhaps didn't seem like such a startling occurrence to an outsider, but Dougal knew how much it took for the colonel to open up, especially concerning a woman.

Anise pouted. "Do visit us again, Colonel Austen."

"Yes, do," Lady Cullen agreed.

"We would be delighted to see you again, Colonel." Poppy's tone was at least sincere with Austen, whereas it hadn't been with Dougal.

Edward had already darted out of the dining room, perhaps afraid his wife would grip him in her talons and not let him escape.

Austen and Dougal followed him out front, where the groomsmen had already brought around their horses for them to mount. Edward sat on his, looking as uncomfortable as he had at the table. Dougal wanted to feel bad for him, but he also thought Edward had made his bed and was going to have to sleep in it for the duration of his days on Earth.

As they rode through the city to New Club in St. Andrew's Square, Edward didn't say a word. Dougal and Austen exchanged glances, both at a loss as to what to say to the man. Dougal respected his brother-in-law's obvious need for a ride in quiet, but there was no way he would sit in the club and watch him stew.

They dismounted and entered the dimly lit club, passing their hats and coats to a footman. Dougal nodded to Lorne, Duke of Sutherland, where he was having a drink with his mates, Euan, Alec and Malcolm. Those Scots were fierce in the pugilist ring, and Dougal grinned as he recalled last summer when he'd challenged all four of them on the mat. Bloody hell, but that had been a lot of fun.

Edward led them to a darkened corner, away from most patrons. Either because he didn't want their conversations to be overheard or he felt like being antisocial. Dougal couldn't be sure which, but it didn't matter because the moment they took their seats, each ordering a whisky, Dougal jumped into conversation.

"What the hell is going on, Edward?"

Edward blanched and looked up sharply. "Pardon?"

"The melancholy at dinner was more suited for a funeral than a meal."

Austen squirmed a little in his chair and took a long sip of his whisky, signaling for another.

Edward grimaced. "I don't know what you're referring to."

"I'm no' some idiot ye can lie to, man. Even the carpet knew there was something wrong. And let's face it, ye've never defied Mary before."

Austen coughed, nearly choking on his whisky. "If ye'll excuse me, mates, I need to have a chat with someone." And then he was up and gone, flying away as if the enemy was on his heels.

Edward watched the colonel's back, his cheeks red, the flush creeping from his neck. "Poppy and I had a disagreement."

"One that changed the moods of everyone present?" Besides Mary, of course. Dougal wasn't brave enough to say that, not to the viper's husband, even if he was her brother.

"Aye."

"Care to share?"

"Not really." Edward avoided looking at him, draining his whisky in one long swallow.

"Will ye share?"

Edward tapped his cup for another. Then he scrubbed a hand down his face, looking more tired at that moment than Dougal had ever seen him.

"Fine. I can see you're not going to let this go."

"I'm no'."

"Mary is not pleased with my mother and sisters' presence in the house." The eye roll produced by Edward rivaled Mary's. Perhaps they did deserve each other.

"Ah." Dougal was already aware of that. "And what does Mary wish ye to do about it?"

Edward scoffed. "What she wants and what I'm willing to do are two different things."

Dougal waited as patiently as he could for Edward to continue, but the man seemed to be battling his inner demons, words failing him.

"And, so, what have ye decided then?"

"I've suggested to Poppy, nay, I've told Poppy, that they are to retire to the dowager house in the Highlands that my father left to my mother. They are not going to be destitute on my watch."

The last statement had Dougal wondering if that was

what Mary had wished. Saints, but was there no end to her selfish and cruel behavior?

"And did Poppy agree?" Dougal could understand Poppy's desire to argue against her brother's decision. Once they moved to the Highlands, there wouldn't be as much fanfare for Anise's coming out, which he knew from the conversation at the creamery that Anise was looking forward to most. But perhaps Edward would not be so cruel and allow them to remain until the end of the season.

"Of course not, but she's got no choice." Edward chugged his next dram and avoided eye contact.

"Is there more to it than that?"

Edward held his cup up, wriggling it to the server, while Dougal still hadn't finished his first. A better friend he might have told to slow down, but Edward was married to Mary, and she was never an easy person to be associated with. Perhaps it would be easier for him to swallow his sour circumstances if there was a heady sloshing of whisky to dull his senses.

"Poppy believes being consigned to the country before the end of the season is akin to spinsterhood for her and Anise."

Dougal paused. So, Edward was aware of that, and still willing to do it. Quite harsh. "So, the plan is to send them before the end of the season?"

Edward rolled his eyes again. "Not you as well. There's nothing wrong with them going now. Plenty of men in the north who need wives. Plenty of dances to meet them too."

Dougal frowned. It was true that men all over the country married, but for ladies, the place to find a match was during the marriage mart. Sending them to the country would make it ten times harder. Aye, he had been to plenty of country dances, but they weren't as populated nor held as often. In the city, there could be a dozen parties a night. In the country, there were maybe a dozen per season.

Still, the Featherstone lassies were beautiful, charming and talented. If anyone could find a husband, it would be the two of them.

And for some reason, which he didn't want to identify, the idea of Poppy looking for a match made his skin tighten. To think she'd have to try and do so in the Highlands without a proper protector...

"Ye'd send them alone?" Dougal asked.

"The dowager house has staff. They'll hardly be alone." Edward waved away Dougal's concern.

"Where exactly is the dowager house? I dinna recall Mary ever mentioning it."

"Why would she? It's nothing to do with her." Edward scowled and cocked his head, looking at Dougal with great concern. "It's in Skerray. Why are you asking me so many questions?"

Dougal was dumbfounded for a moment. Skerray was near the tip of the highest point of Scotland and only a few hours' walk from his Castle Varrich. He narrowed his eyes, for a moment wondering if this was some trick, but then recalled that the house belonged to Lady Cullen, left to her by her husband as her dower property and that the late Lord Leven had links to that northernmost part of the country had been partly why Mary and Edward were matched in the first place. Mutual invested properties.

"Curiosity. Considering the two younger ladies had different designs on their season when I took them for iced cream earlier today." Dougal shrugged, pretending as if it wasn't any matter to him.

Edward scowled, clearly not believing him. "Why did you do that?"

"Do what?" Now it was Dougal's turn to scowl. He felt as if he were being accused of something, though he couldn't say what.

"Take them out. You're under no obligation to do so. Why did you?"

Dougal could hardly say it was because Mary was a tyrant. As deep as Edward was drowning in his cups, he was liable to punch him in the face if he did. "Why not?"

"Mary thinks you're getting too close." Edward wagged his finger, though the whisky was starting to take effect, and it looked a little more like a wiggle.

Perhaps if he played dumb long enough, Edward would simply pass out. "Too close to what?"

"My sisters."

Dougal shrugged. "I thought I was being polite." It was more than he could say for their brother, who was distancing himself from the family he'd been given charge of.

"Perhaps their well-being is none of your business?" Edward set down his empty whisky cup a little harder than he should have, drawing the attention of a few club members nearby.

Dougal paused a moment, considering. Edward was likely right, except that he did care, and it felt like he might be the only one who did right now.

"Another!" Edward bellowed to the footman, who wasn't moving quickly enough with the crystal decanter.

"Perhaps ye've had enough," Dougal suggested, giving a hand signal for the footman to wait.

Edward leaned forward, perfecting a Mary bearing of the teeth. "Stay out of my business and away from my family."

Dougal set down his whisky and leaned forward. "Ye forget, Edward, that Mary *is* my family."

The scoff from Edward sounded more like a snort he might choke on. "She's no longer your responsibility."

"Verra true." Dougal stood. "And I can see ye're doing a brilliant job of taking care of your responsibilities."

"A man ought not to judge another man." Edward's words were slurred, and Dougal felt only disgust for his brother-in-law.

He refrained from saying, "I see no man here," and instead said, "A man ought no' to give cause for judgment."

He walked away from Edward, the idiot cursing behind him, and then he found Austen, who was deep in a game of billiards. He wished his friend well and then walked toward the exit, needing fresh air.

He slipped the host a pound note at the front of the club. "Dinna let that one back on his horse." He indicated to where Edward was bellowing for more whisky. "He's liable to break his neck."

"Aye, my lord."

Dougal rode the long way home, still feeling as though he was in the dark. Aye, he understood the melancholy now from dinner. The three ladies were being banished and displaced, their lives and dreams upended. Hardly seemed fair.

Rather than ride to his house, he stopped in front of Edward and Mary's residence. All the windows were lit up, but by now, they would have finished dinner—which he was still starving from having missed.

A lone face appeared in the window of an upper story.

Poppy.

Their eyes met behind the glass. She stared down at him, not bothering to shut the curtains or wave. And then she disappeared. He really ought to leave. Perhaps Edward was right that it was none of his business, but something inside him compelled him to stay. He wanted to help.

Not that there was much he could do. They were Edward's responsibility. They would go to Skerray, and there, they would begin a new life.

But still, their brother was being unnecessarily cruel, and it stank of Mary's vindictiveness. Maybe a talk with his sister might help. But not at this hour. Mary was best in the mornings before she'd had a chance to energize herself by sucking the joy from everyone throughout the entire day.

Dougal started to ride off when the front door of the house opened, and Poppy, wrapped in a shawl, sauntered out toward the gate. She looked ethereal, mysterious and beautiful in the glow of the streetlamps. He couldn't seem to stop staring, nor could he form words.

"What are you doing here?" she asked. "Shouldn't you be at the club with my brother?"

Dougal chuckled. "I'd rather not watch while he drinks himself under. Besides, he was being a bit of a..." How could he put it delicately?

"Arse?" She nodded. "He was that way with me as well."

Dougal wished there were a way he could comfort her. "Ah, I'm sorry."

"Not your fault."

"Nay, 'tis no', but that doesna mean I dinna feel sorry all the same. Ye dinna deserve it."

She shook her head. "I just don't understand. I'm assuming you know now what Edward has decided."

Dougal nodded, his lips turned down. "He told me. I dinna understand why he decided, but I do know my sister is relentless."

"She hates us and is clearly behind Edward's decision. We're just lucky he's letting Mama keep the dower house when Mary wanted him to—" She cut herself off, sucking her bottom lip into her mouth with a deep inhale. Then she let it out slowly. "Sorry, I've said too much."

"I dinna think 'tis hate."

Poppy gave him a look that said, "You obviously are missing a few marbles in the head."

"Mary is never satisfied with Mary. Most of her actions, words and thoughts all stem from deep insecurities. Anything she does to harm ye is only reflected back on her."

"So, you're saying we make her feel less than?" Poppy cocked her head, looking perplexed and thoughtful.

"Aye. Ye are all beautiful, charming women. This was your mother's house years ago. She used to run the household. Likely, some of the servants are still listening to her. And even if that's all in Mary's head, it still lives there, eating away at her."

"That was a lifetime ago for Mama. And Anise and I have never lived in this house. That is silly."

"Still, she feels your mother's mark on it." Dougal shrugged. "Mary was never good at sharing and certainly no' good at having anyone's leavings."

"I think she wants our dowries."

"How so?" He wrinkled his brow.

"If we are not married by a certain age, the dowries revert to the heirs." She lowered her gaze, staring at his horse's hooves. "I shouldn't be telling you all this. And even if the heirs are not in Edward's line since we don't share a father, Mary's scheming to figure out a way, as he's the executor, to charge us rent from those assets."

Dougal's chest tightened, and though he tried hard not to show any outward effect at Mary's games, the vein in his neck throbbed. "I'll not say a word."

"My mother is devasted, and Anise…" Poppy sighed. "She feels as if she's being sentenced to death."

"Social death."

Poppy looked up at him, her expression saying she was surprised he understood. "It is very much like that."

"Edward says the dower house is in Skerray."

Poppy nodded, holding her shawl closer to ward off a brisk wind sweeping the street.

"I dinna think it is as bleak as ye think."

"No?"

Dougal shook his head. "Nay, my lady. I've got a residence nearby myself."

She looked up at him then, surprised, and something stirred in Dougal's chest. Was that a little spark of hope in her eyes?

"I often go there in the off seasons, and the neighbors are all pleasant. There's a village as well for shopping and even a little creamery."

"Truly?"

"Aye. 'Tis no' Edinburgh, but 'tis no' as bleak as ye may think. Though, dinna say anything to Mary about that. Sounds as though she wishes to put ye all into the woods and leave ye there."

"Aye, I think she might if given the chance."

"Dinna give up hope. Your life is going to change, but no' for the worse. Just different."

Poppy smiled. It was a sad curve of her pretty pink lips, but also a little hopeful. "Thank you for telling me." She opened her mouth again, looking as though she might say something else, but a loud tapping on glass interrupted them both.

Dougal looked up at the house and saw his sister knocking against the window on an upper level, her face stern as ever. If she tapped any harder, she might very well shatter the window, raining shards down on them both. How long had she been standing there? Had she heard anything that they'd said? Saints, but he hoped not, or there would be bloody hell to pay.

"The dragon sweeps in," he murmured. "She never played nice as a child. And I'm afraid no' much has changed since then."

Poppy laughed. The sound was a stark difference from how she'd sounded when she first came outside. "I'd best go before she storms out here and incinerates us both."

"Good idea. Though do be careful inside. I'd no' be surprised if she lit ye up once ye closed the door."

Poppy shuddered, and though it was meant to be exaggerated and playful, he sensed a small part of it was real. Not because she was scared of Mary but because anyone dealing with his sister had no other recourse but a physical one to let out the frustration of every encounter.

Dougal watched her retreat, hoping at least he had lightened the bleak outlook she had and ignoring why he wanted to.

Poppy closed the door behind her, but Mary remained in the window, staring at him without moving a muscle.

Bloody hell. He was going to pay for this, he could tell.

❧ 7 ❧

As soon as the door closed behind Poppy, Mary marched across the foyer floor, heels clicking against the marble in ominous *tap-tap-tap-taps*. Her steps were so loud and hard that Poppy wouldn't have been surprised if her sister-in-law's heels left impressions in the hard stone, little divots as reminders of her ire.

"What do you think you're doing?" Mary's tone was full of bitter accusations.

Poppy closed her eyes, drawing in a breath, trying to find her center so that when she turned around, she could look halfway pleasant rather than as put out as she felt.

"Poppy Featherstone, I'm speaking to you."

Oh, angels above, please help me have patience. Poppy turned around, a smile forced onto her mouth. "A word with a friend."

"Friend?" Mary's pinched features looked ready to crack, and she rocked back on her heels as if Poppy's very words had pushed her off balance. "Dougal is no *friend* of yours. He's my brother."

"And you are my sister-in-law. Married to my brother.

Stands to reason we are all close, does it not?" So close, Poppy could feel the singe of Mary's fire.

"Stay away from Dougal." Mary straightened, the anger in her features changing to a smug satisfaction. "He's attached. No use wasting your time there."

Attached? Mary might as well have kicked her shoe right into Poppy's face. But years of dealing with her sister-in-law and the *ton* had taught her to hide her feelings properly. Poppy didn't even flinch; the surprise of that revelation only affected her on the inside. Dougal was *attached*. Was that why he'd left town so abruptly last season?

Then why had he kissed her? Anger started to diffuse the surprise. He'd...used her.

"That's right," Mary continued as if Poppy had reacted and asked for confirmation. "Lucia Steventon. They've been betrothed for several years."

Several? So, not last season? How was it that the engagement had never been announced? Poppy felt her face drain of color, the blood from her head quickly whizzing down her other limbs.

"Lucia's been abroad," Mary continued, digging the knife in deeper, the smirk on her face saying she knew how much she was hurting Poppy with every word. "Her father was an attaché in Spain. Their wedding is sure to come before the end of the season."

Poppy managed a smile feeling as brittle as the porcelain she hadn't taken her tea in, and kept her voice light as she replied, "How lovely."

It was absolutely imperative that she not let Mary know how much this news crushed her. Though considering her current light-headedness and obvious pallor, she was certain her sister-in-law already knew.

When Dougal had shared that he had a house near the

79

dower cottage in the Highlands, it felt as if he'd let her know there was a chance they might be together, or at the very least that she wouldn't be alone. That she, her sister and mother would have the company of a good friend.

But an engagement meant something different. It meant not just Dougal as a neighbor but his wife. Lucia Steventon, whom Poppy had never heard of nor seen before. Poppy's heart cracked behind her ribs, and her lungs burned for the need to suck in air. The longer she stood here, the more likely she wouldn't be able to escape.

"It is very lovely. Lucia is a wonderful lady and quite accomplished." Mary continued blathering on as if she wanted to add rusted edges to the metaphorical knife she'd stabbed through Poppy's heart.

Poppy nodded, her smile now as frozen in place as her locked knees. "I'd be delighted to meet her, but as it turns out, I'll be away in the Highlands. Shame."

Mary smiled now, well pleased. Everything she wanted was coming true with absolutely no reason why. She was getting rid of the Featherstones and really sticking it to them. As if Poppy, Anise and their mother had offended Mary somehow, when all they'd ever been was kind. "That's right, you're leaving in the morning, aren't you?"

"Quite right." That was *not* right at all. Her brother hadn't given her an exact departure before, only that it would need to be soon and before the end of the season. She'd thought they might have a week to prepare, but now it appeared the time had been set for her by Mary. And considerably moved up. That was hardly...

"Shame, I was hoping to have another dinner with Colonel Austen. He seemed keen on Anise." Mary shrugged. "Oh well, perhaps when you all visit sometime next year."

Banished for at least a year from this house. Poppy swallowed back her anger and tears, which were clawing their way up her throat, begging to be hollered out.

"Perhaps," she said, though it came out sounding rather strangled.

"Good night, Poppy," Mary said her name like a sneer as if the two syllables were meant to sting.

Poppy didn't respond but gave Mary her back. There was no reason for her to be cordial to the woman now. Not when she'd practically tossed them on their arses into the streets. There were so many things Poppy wanted to say, none of them good. And she knew it was best to walk away before she said something she regretted.

"I said, '*Good night*, Poppy.'" Mary's pitch increased, the disrespect one of the only weapons Poppy ever had to wield. Mary couldn't handle not being treated exactly as she should be.

Poppy continued up the stairs, pretending she hadn't heard her.

"Poppy!" The shriek was so loud Poppy swore the windows rattled.

Still, she ignored the wench and turned around the corner of the corridor at the top, out of sight. She'd not made it six inches out view before she sucked in a massive gulp of air. Mary threw an epic tantrum in the foyer, screaming for Edward before realizing he was not in residence. A few doors from the servant's quarters sounded, and then rushing footsteps. Likely the poor servants believed there was an emergency. Poor things, having to deal with Mary.

Poppy made it to her room at the same time Anise flung open their door, and their mother across the hallway opened hers. They both looked stricken and frightened.

"What's happened?" their mother asked, eyes flicking

toward the stairs where the shrieks had pierced the air seconds ago.

"Mary has informed me we're leaving for the dower house tomorrow morning."

"Tomorrow?" Anise's face crumpled. "I've not even had a chance to tell my friends."

"I will appeal to Edward." Mama's hand trembled where she held the door, her face paling just as Poppy's had. "He must give us time. We've not even begun to pack."

Poppy hugged her mother and pressed a kiss to her temple. "We will be all right, Mama. I think it best we not spend another minute in this house with that..."

"Bitch?" Anise offered.

"I think that's an offense to bitches everywhere," their mother said, surprising them both.

Poppy clapped a hand over her mouth, and Anise took a step back into their room, covering her mouth to keep her laugh from being heard by the very bitch in question.

"I love you, Mama," Poppy said.

"And I you, both of you. Now, get some sleep. It appears we've got a long adventure tomorrow."

The following morning, servants arrived with trunks and guilty expressions before they'd even risen, knocking on the doors just past dawn. Their maid whispered how sorry she was to be packing their things, and the footmen who carried the trunks looked forlorn as they disappeared with all the Featherstone belongings.

Poppy descended the stairs so quickly that she thought she might trip and fall in search of her brother. Thank goodness there was no sight yet of Mary. Rather than prowling the halls looking for people to bite, she must have decided to sleep in. Or stay out of their way now that she was getting what she wanted.

The dining room was empty. As was Edward's study. Not even the faint scent of his aftershave to suggest he'd been there recently.

"Where is Lord Leven?" she asked the butler, Grant, who'd been in her brother's service for as long as she could remember. He'd come to the townhouse when Edward had inherited it, and when they'd first been given residence after Papa died, Poppy had been glad for the familiarity and a possible ally.

The butler, too polite to say anything, conveyed quite a lot in his apologetic expression. "I believe he stayed overnight at his club, my lady." He glanced around, perhaps expecting Mary to burst through a wall. Perhaps she wasn't here at all. Maybe they would be lucky enough that she'd left from the house in search of her husband, and they wouldn't have to see her. "This came for ye, Miss Anise and Lady Cullen."

Grant held out a small white envelope, the kind that usually held a calling card. On the front, in a neat scroll, was written: *Lady Cullen and the Misses Featherstone.*

Her heart clenched to know this would be the last card they got in Edinburgh. Unless their circumstances changed, she highly doubted they would be returning. Poppy opened the envelope, praying at once that it was Dougal's card and, at the very same time, that it wasn't. On the one hand, she wanted him to come and explain his secret engagement, or at least why he'd failed to mention it. Especially right before he'd kissed her, so she might have had the choice not to press her lips to his... Though in the state she'd been, would she have had the nerve to deny him? She wanted to ask why he'd flirted shamelessly with her and given her hope that they might be a possible match when he'd already been tethered to another. But the name inside was not Dougal Mackay.

Instead, it was Sir John Ross. The young gentlemen they'd met at the creamery.

The one she'd rather hoped might forget he'd wanted to call. Poppy let out a disappointed sigh.

"And this one."

The butler handed her another card, this one from Colonel Austen. While his card was welcome, it was Dougal's she had been hoping to see.

"Are there any others?" Though she tried not to seem sad about it, she was certain she sounded pitiful.

"I'm afraid no', miss." The butler shook his head, looking as disheartened as she felt.

She nodded, swallowing her disappointment, shoving away all her questions and frustration with Dougal, not wanting to think about whether she'd ever get the chance to voice them.

"Should I send a reply to your inquiries?"

Poppy nodded. "For this morning, please, if they can make it, so we might say goodbye before we are thrust into an uncertain future. I do believe Lady Leven will have our carriage around as soon as she wakes for us to depart. We've got a long journey."

Days, really. Maybe even a week on the road, even with their horse and carriage going full speed, which wouldn't be possible in the Highlands.

The butler, stoic at all times, flinched now. "I would go with ye if they'd allow it," he said softly. "Pardon my being so forward."

"I wish you could."

"I'll have Cook pack the lot of ye something extra fine for your journey."

"Thank you, Grant. I appreciate that, as I'm sure my mother and Anise will as well."

Poppy returned upstairs to where the servants were still packing their things. Anise was sobbing at her dressing table while Mama brushed her hair.

"We have two gentleman callers coming this morning before we depart," Poppy said. "So, dry your eyes. No need for them to see you puffy."

"Who is it?" Anise asked, the very picture of sadness as she stared up watery eyed at Poppy through the looking glass.

"Colonel Austen and Sir John."

Anise perked up at the latter name. She swiped at the tears with a handkerchief and managed a smile. "Oh, how wonderful. Perhaps we can ask them to visit us in the Highlands?"

"I don't think it would hurt to suggest they call if they are in the area, but we must do so carefully," their mother said, showing more energy than she had in months.

"I will follow your lead, Mama," Anise said.

Poppy sat down on the chaise longue, watching her mother and sister prepare for their visitors, feeling sorry for herself, for the one person she wanted to see wasn't coming and had apparently lied to her. Perhaps about more than one thing. He'd certainly toyed with her affections.

"What is it, Pop?" Anise asked, coming to sit beside her and pulling her hands onto her lap.

Poppy didn't know whether she should say it aloud. Doing so made it seem more real, which was the last thing she wanted. Giving credence to Mary's venom felt like a betrayal to her own self. But then again, if they were all going to be sad about one thing or another, they should know that there was no hope for her and the man she'd hoped to marry one day. "Dougal is engaged."

"Engaged?" Her mother turned around, her expression as shocked as Poppy felt. "To whom?"

"Lucia Steventon."

"Since when?" Anise gaped.

"I don't know." This part was true. Yes, Mary had said for several years, but who knew whether that was an exaggeration or not? The truth was she had no facts other than what her sister-in-law had spewed.

"I thought..." Anise trailed off, not voicing the hopes that Poppy had cherished until Mary incinerated them last night.

That there was a future somewhere over the crest of the next hill for her and Dougal. That they just needed more time together for him to get down on one knee and offer her a lifetime. But those were silly notions of a naïve girl. A stupid, idiot debutante who'd let a flirtation get too carried away for her own good and ended up kissing a man she'd thought loved her.

There'd been no declarations. Nothing but champagne and heat and desire all wrapped up into one swirling, delicious disaster. And now she had the broken heart to prove what a fool she'd been.

"I thought so too." Poppy shrugged, hardening her heart, and forcing herself not to feel anything. No anger. No pain. Nothing at all.

Perhaps Dougal's prior attachment to Lucia was for the best. As she'd quickly found out, being in love or ruled over by a spouse could make a person into someone no one respected. And quite frankly, that sounded awful.

I am not Edward.

And she never would be.

No one will rule over me but myself.

8

"**M**y lord, a missive has arrived for ye. The footman claimed it was urgent."

Dougal glanced up from where he'd been working on ledgers in his study to find his butler holding out a small white card on a silver tray. He always thought the silver tray was silly. As if paper could not be passed between servant and lord, but rather needed to be placed on something expensive first.

"Thank ye, James." Dougal took the small white envelope. The decisive letters of his name looped in black ink. The penmanship was not one he recognized, and given the urgency of the contents, he felt a little apprehensive about opening it.

Dougal tore open the missive, and read the contents once, twice, then a third time for good measure.

My lord,

Begging your pardon for stepping out of bounds, but I thought you would like to know that Lady Leven has requested the packing and removal of the Featherstone ladies to the Highlands this morning. Their departure is imminent.

Respectfully,

Mr. Grant

Butler to Lord Leven

Dougal growled under his breath, feeling as if this sudden change in the course of events was his fault. If he'd not stopped and talked to Poppy last night, there might have still been time to convince his sister to let them remain in Edinburgh, at least until the end of the season, to give them time to find suitable matches.

There also remained the question of why his presence would prompt his sister into such action unless she feared Poppy might interfere with his engagement to Lucia Steventon, and if that were the case, why would Mary be so invested in the young lady? They didn't know each other as far as he knew. Then again, perhaps this was just one of Mary's machinations without an understandable motive. No matter—if he didn't leave now, he might miss their imminent departure, and then he'd kick himself the entire ride up the road to intercept them.

"James, have the carriage brought around. And send a letter north letting them know I'll be arriving within the week, so they need to have the castle opened."

"Aye, my lord."

Dougal crumpled the note and tossed it into the rubbish bin. It wasn't unusual for him to go to his sister's residence, and often, he arrived for breakfast, much to her chagrin. So, he didn't suspect she would have instructed her butler to slam the door in his face—though given it was Grant who'd written the missive, the man would at least do it with regrets. And fortunately, Dougal was right. Rather than him being barred from the residence, Grant let him in with a nod of respect.

"My lord," Grant said, eyeing him warily. "The ladies are receiving guests in the drawing room."

"So early?"

Grant nodded. "They are to depart just after luncheon." He leaned closer and whispered, "Though my lady wished it to have been after breakfast."

"I appreciate the warning, Grant. Ye're a loyal man."

"Others may no' think so." The butler walked toward the drawing room and opened the door, the ladies' voices filtering into the grand foyer. Grant announced Dougal, which brought a hush from the women but a "Hey-ho!" from Colonel Austen, whom he was particularly surprised to see.

Poppy looked up sharply, her eyes narrowing upon seeing him on the threshold of the drawing room. Though she tried to mask her surprise, there was a slight quiver to her lower lip that he wished to quell, though he had no right. There was anger and hurt there, and while he hadn't done anything more to her since leaving her in London, it felt as if she were directly accusing him of something. She was probably resentful that Mary had moved up their departure, which was entirely his fault. Or was it something deeper? *Mo chreach*, but he wished he could ask her *without* an audience present.

Dougal bowed. Anise was sitting between Colonel Austen and Sir John on a couch that appeared dwarfed by the two men on either side. If Austen was a surprise, Sir John was even more so. How had that fool ingratiated himself to the ladies so quickly to have garnered an invitation? Sir John was a bastard and not to be trusted, and Dougal was having a hard time holding in the growl he wanted to let out.

Poppy perched beside her mother, hands folded in her lap, though with how her knuckles were white from her grip, she was not seated comfortably. There was no sign of Mary—thank goodness—which he found to be surprising. Mary wouldn't normally have wanted to miss this for the world. Especially the sad goodbyes that were a result of her machinations. Not to mention that she would want to mess up any pleasantries.

"Lord Reay," the dowager said rather coldly. He'd not been on the frosty side of her attention before now. Something had definitely changed overnight, and he didn't think his evening drop-in was the reason. "A surprise to see you this morning, sir."

It wasn't, really. He'd been there most mornings since they'd arrived, but the coldness was clear. He was being blamed. He wasn't invited. He was an interloper. An outsider in this new, small assembly.

"I do apologize for not sending a card," he said. "I wanted to come and"—

he glanced at Poppy, locking his gaze on hers—"apologize for any inconvenience I may have caused."

Colonel Austen eyed him oddly, and Sir John too. At least those two had no idea why he was being shunned. Though, honestly, he'd liked to have known himself, and if they were aware, they might all discuss it in the open.

"What inconvenience is that?" Poppy cocked her head as if she dared him to put voice to her ire, the very reason she suddenly despised him.

They'd been making progress, he thought...

Dougal swallowed. He wasn't normally one to feel nervous in any situation, but heaven help him. Poppy made him feel unsettled, uncontrolled, and out of his depth. "Might I ask for your company on a walk about the garden, Miss Featherstone?" He directed his question at Poppy.

Poppy glanced toward Anise as if seeking confirmation,

then back at Dougal. "I'm sorry, I think I'd rather not catch a chill, sir. You're welcome to join us here or perhaps come calling later this afternoon, after luncheon, though I doubt the chill will be gone. Oh, gracious me, I forgot we won't be here this afternoon." She let out a laugh that he saw through for what it was. She mocked him. "And likely neither should you, Lord Reay." Her steely gaze met his, and there was a turn to her lips that was partly cruel and partly wounded. She was lashing out. "Perhaps your fiancée would much rather you take her for a walk about?"

Dougal's mouth went dry. It appeared he'd stepped in it twice. Not only was he responsible for them leaving early, but Mary had clearly shared Lucia's imminent arrival, though she hadn't shared all of the information—like how he didn't consider himself to be betrothed. Everything made sense now. Her anger, her hurt, Lady Cullen's coldness, Anise agreeing she shouldn't walk with him in the garden. They believed him to be some rogue.

And my God, hadn't he proven himself to be exactly that?

Still, Dougal pressed on. He wasn't going to let her go without explaining what the situation was. There were always two sides to every story, and didn't he deserve a chance to share his? "Might we have a word in confidence?"

Poppy rolled her eyes, and Colonel Austen shifted uncomfortably in his chair while Sir John looked as if he wanted this theatre entertainment to go on for a while longer, perhaps with refreshments brought in.

For as much as she put on a show, Poppy's curiosity appeared to get the better of her. And he was grateful.

She stood and marched over to him. The gentle sway of her hips was taken over by her irritation. "We can speak in the corner here, but I will not leave this room with you, and under no circumstances will I be alone with you again. It wouldn't be proper. And I'll not have any more rumors tossed around society about me." She trooped toward the corner, beckoning with a flick of her hand for him to follow.

While he would have rather spoken to her privately, he would take whatever he got from Poppy, even the corner of the drawing room with all eyes on them.

She folded her arms across her chest but thankfully did not tap her foot as he might have expected. "What is it that you wish to say, Lord Reay?"

Anger radiated from her in waves, and he felt guilty for so many reasons. The repeated use of his titled name put distance between them, as if erasing the friendship they'd had...the kiss they'd shared. The way he'd wanted her so badly that his insides ached, and then fear had made him run away. Afraid he'd not be able to give her all she deserved.

Dougal cleared his throat, adjusting the cravat that suddenly felt too tight at his neck. "I am no' betrothed, no' really."

She cocked an eyebrow at him. "And I'm not going to the country, not really. My heart will always remain in Edinburgh." Sarcasm dripped from her words in streams like the wax of a hundred candles on a single chandelier.

"I'd like to explain if ye'll allow me."

She waved her hand, impatient.

"'Twas an adolescent proposal." There, he'd said it. He breathed out a sigh of relief.

But Poppy's expression didn't change. "Did you ask her to marry you?"

"Aye," he drawled out, not sure where she was going with her questions.

Poppy, too, drawled out her words as if she hoped he'd pick up on whatever she was thinking. "And did she say yes?"

"Aye." Dougal shook his head. "But we were young."

Poppy let out a sharp laugh. A quick succession of *ha-ha*. "I don't think the age matters much if the two of you have consented to marry."

"But I do no' wish to marry her. I've never had any intentions of marrying her." How could he make her understand?

"Sounds as if you have a problem then, Lord Reay. And as much as I thought we were friends, we are not. And I have my own problems, namely the fact that my brother has betrayed me and we are being forced to move to the Highlands in the middle of the season, and I will have to help my sister transition to a desolate life that she doesn't want. Two spinsters and their widowed mother. It all sounds so trite, and yet it is my new life."

The bitter ache of her words cut through his solar plexus. He wanted to wrap her in his arms, to tell her that he would not let that happen, that she and Anise were too young and beautiful to be spinsters, that even her mother could find happiness. But he could tell by the way she looked at him that anything he said would go in one ear and be tossed in the trash from the other.

"My lady, please allow me to try and make this right." He was mucking this up royally.

"And how do you expect to do that?" Now Poppy's foot did tap, and she looked over his shoulder at the group, her cheeks flushing a light shade of pink.

Dougal dared not look behind him but judging by the overly chipper and volume of Anise's voice, she was trying to get everyone's attention back on her. And then, thankfully, the tinny notes of the piano sounded, drowning their words into the music and away from prying ears.

"I will speak with Mary," he said. "Tell her to see sense."

"That will never happen." Poppy's voice was full of venom, and she rolled her eyes. "Mary and sense are complete opposites. And to be frank, I don't want to spend another minute in this house with her. She is cruel and unkind. We deserve to be treated better. And my brother..." She shook her head, her voice trailing off as it cracked with emotion.

Everything she said was true. They didn't deserve Mary's treatment. None of it. Mary had not changed since she was a child. Back then, if another child wanted to play with her dolls, she didn't only snatch them back and not share—she also destroyed the dolls so even she could not play with them.

The Featherstones were her dolls. And she was tearing them up right now. Gouging them with pins and cutting them with metaphorical scissors.

Dougal had done a lot throughout their lives to hide Mary's true nature from the world. And when she'd found a partner in Edward, Dougal had been relieved to see that the man was truly infatuated with her. That her cruelness did not extend to the man she loved, and somehow, maybe she'd changed. A miracle, really.

But, as it turned out, she must have found the only other person in this world who destroyed their treasures too. Two peas in a pod they were, and Lord help their son to make it through unscathed.

The cross of her arms shifted, and she held her arms beneath the shoulders, hugging herself rather than shutting him out. Dougal swallowed against the ache in his chest.

"Why are you so..." Poppy shook her head, not finishing her sentence, but Dougal could guess what she was asking.

Why was he so invested? He didn't have an answer to that. Perhaps it was inappropriate for him to extend the interest, the concern. But he was human, and what human didn't empathize with another in pain? Especially when he knew his sister was the reason for their hurt.

But there was more to it than that.

When Dougal looked into Poppy's fiery eyes, something inside him that he had long thought dead lit up. It was why he'd pursued her in London and why he'd run from her.

It was why he'd come to Edinburgh to begin with. Why he was here now.

And he knew his actions confused her; they confounded even himself. But he couldn't walk away from her. Not for his inheritance, Lucia, Mary or society itself. At this moment, looking at her usually straight spine curving in on itself, Dougal would have given up everything if only to help her stand up tall again.

"I'm sorry," he said, and he meant it from the deepest part of himself. The urge to pull her into his arms was strong. He started to lift his hands, then let them drop. With an audience present, he dared not touch her, even if his entire body urged him forward.

Without the impending arrival of Lucia, of her calling in on a promise made a decade before, could there have been something more between Poppy and him? A war between sense—Poppy—and sensibility—Lucia—waged inside him. He knew which side he was on; he just didn't know how to get there.

"I am, too," she said, with a small shake of her head, no longer meeting his gaze.

And then she did the thing he'd feared most. She turned around and walked away. She didn't return to her seat at tea but continued through the door of the drawing room out into the grand foyer. The door closed behind her with a gentle snick.

Dougal wasn't certain he'd ever see her again. And the very idea of that snapped his heart in two.

9

Poppy held herself together until she entered her bedchamber and went through to the dressing room. Then she shut the door, sank to the floor behind a few dresses that had yet to be gathered, and the dam of tears burst.

Long, rushing floods of salty water dripped down her face. She pressed her hands to her mouth, trying to muffle the sobs escaping her throat as her shoulders racked, rattling the wall behind her.

For so long, she'd believed that a life with Dougal was just a flirtation away. That she just needed to prove herself worthy of him somehow. That he'd been called away from London on some important business and if she were just patient enough, he would come back, all apologies.

But a year had gone by with hardly a word about him.

And when he'd arrived in Edinburgh, she'd had even begun to hope once more that they could rekindle the romance they'd started the year before. He was attentive, concerned and flirtatious. They'd seemed to pick up right where they left off. And her heart, which she'd tried to harden against him, had opened up and allowed him to infiltrate her defenses once more.

And now, all of that was dashed. There was another woman, a lady who had already staked her claim. Whom he'd asked to marry him. More fool her.

Mary was cruel, and yet somehow, Dougal's cruelty hurt worse. A fiancée all this time? Every flirtation, the kiss, all of it was a game. Perhaps even a joke he'd laughed about with friends at the club. Though, to be fair to Colonel Austen, she didn't see him behaving in that way.

At least Mary wore her meanness on her sleeve. Dougal kept his locked up tight, a shadow that slithered up behind you and stabbed you in the back.

A soft knock sounded at the dressing room door.

Poppy squeezed her eyes shut and held her breath, hoping whoever was on the other side would go away. She didn't ever let anyone see her in a state like this. And she certainly wasn't going to start now. Pulling her handkerchief from her sleeve, she swiped frantically at her tears and her dripping nose. She couldn't remain hidden all day, and she wouldn't let anyone see her looking so ridiculous.

Broken heart or not, she had to stand tall.

"Poppy?" Anise's tone was full of concern. "Sir John and the colonel have gone. They say they'll visit us in the Highlands once we've settled."

Poppy swiped angrily at the tears on her cheeks that refused to cease falling despite her orders. She pushed herself to her feet. At least it was only Anise on the other side of the door. Her sister wasn't one to judge, even if she was a bit headstrong and silly sometimes.

Poppy flung open the door and stared at Anise, daring her to mention that her face was likely blotchy from sobbing, her eyes red and swollen. Her dripping nose making it seem as if her face had become a waterfall.

Anise stared at her, mouth open, not hiding the horror of what she saw. Thankfully, however, she didn't say anything. Just grabbed Poppy, wrapping her in her arms and squeezing her tight. They were close but did not often hug. At first, Poppy stiffened, putting her hands up to push her sister off. But rather than push, she pulled, hugging her just as tight. Needing the feeling of closeness, of being held, more than she'd realized.

Needing to know that someone was on her side. That maybe everything would be all right even if it felt as if her life was an utter disaster.

Even after their father died, they'd hugged but not clung like this.

"Papa is gone, and our lives are changing," Anise whispered, her voice tight with emotion. "Again. But that doesn't mean our lives are over, Poppy. We'll make the best of it. We'll be all right. I promise."

Poppy had said something very similar just last night.

"We will rebuild. We'll be the belles of the Highlands, and Mary can take her snooty self and shove it up her arse."

Poppy laughed, sniffling from her running nose. "And Edward too."

"He's no brother of mine," Anise declared. "Except when I want that dowry."

"If Mary hasn't figured out a way to confiscate it first."

"Ugh, I hate her." Anise pulled back a moment, frowning, her eyes searching Poppy's.

"I hate her too. With a passion that might rival the gods at war."

"Who are we hating?" their mother asked as she breezed

into the room and popped the dressing room door open further.

"Oh, Mama, wild guess?" Poppy said, finally letting go of her sister.

"No need to be wild about it. Half of Edinburgh is already talking about her and what she's done, and the other half will be by the end of the day." Mama clucked her tongue as if she'd already had a letter to confirm the information.

"Are they?" Anise asked, rubbing her hands together.

Their mother nodded, waving a handful of notes. "Oh, yes, dear ones. My friends are making sure Mary's actions make the rounds. They said as much in their farewells and promises to visit, along with their cleverly disguised insults to Mary and her vindictiveness."

Anise grabbed their mother's hand and dragged her toward the chaise longue, tugging her down to sit. "Give us one juicy insult, Mama, so we can walk out of the house with our heads held high."

Poppy clicked the lock on their bedroom door so no one could interrupt.

"All right, my dears, I'd be happy to oblige. But not out here. We need the protection of one more door." Mama hurried them into the dressing room and shut that door too. Poppy and Anise waited, breath held. "Lady Sutherland says, 'I'll be sure to send all of my invitations with the name Featherstone and Cullen to your residence in the Highlands and lament about you not being able to come on account of it being so far and shall wipe the name Leven from my book.'"

"My goodness." Poppy's mouth fell open. "Lady Sutherland is like a queen around here. And she is all but saying Mary will be shunned from society."

"It does seem that way, doesn't it?" their mother nodded, her face serious but her eyes dancing.

"One more, Mama?"

"I'll not fill your heads with idle gossip, but do know that most of my correspondence reads like such. And I think we will not want for company in the country, as many have suggested ending their seasons early to come north."

Poppy watched her sister's shoulders sag with relief. And while knowing that at least they weren't being tossed to the ends of the earth for quiet nonexistence, she was still devastated for other reasons.

"What did Dougal have to say?" Anise asked, not pulling any punches.

Poppy shrugged, not wanting to discuss it, still feeling the pain of it all so deeply inside, like a festering wound that would not heal.

"Don't shrug, dear. It's not good for your posture." Mama tapped her shoulders.

Poppy managed to roll her eyes without her mother seeing. "Nothing he can say will change the facts. Nor our departure. He offered to speak to Mary on our behalf to convince her otherwise, but we all know how that would turn out."

"I meant about the engagement. Is it true?" Anise's eyes locked on hers, and Poppy couldn't look away.

"It is true. He claims to have been young and impulsive and that he had no intention of following through on his proposal, and yet here the lady comes from abroad to walk down the aisle. Everyone seemed to know about it but me." Poppy groaned. "I'm such a fool. I should have forgotten about him the moment he left London last year."

"Shame he can't break it off." Anise pursed her lips. "The folly of youth should not have to be paid for. Unless, of course, it's a crime. And I think a youthful proposal is not a crime. And how unfair that it is you being punished for it."

Poppy sighed and shrugged, which got her another tap on the shoulders by her mother. "He won't back out of the proposal as that would be dishonorable, even if his heart is not in it. Dougal is honorable." *To a degree*.

"To a fault," Anise muttered and shook her head. "He would give up on what you two had for some ancient person in his life?"

"It appears so." Mama stroked a finger over Poppy's arm.

If he were truly an honorable man, he wouldn't have flirted with her—kissed her—when he was already engaged to someone else. Perhaps this forced move was a blessing in disguise. Dougal had broken her heart, but if their relationship had progressed any further, she would have been crushed body and soul to find out that he'd committed himself to another.

Even thinking about it made her lightheaded.

And all of a sudden, escaping to the Highlands felt like the most perfect thing they should do. To get away from the humiliation of thinking herself in love with a man already claimed by another. For escaping a sister-in-law who hated her, and a brother who was indifferent.

"We shall find you both husbands in the Highlands. And for you, Poppy dear, one who is not already engaged," her mother said matter-of-factly. Poppy ignored that her mother implied she'd tried to marry a man already spoken for, for she knew that wasn't what her mother meant. "There are plenty of men in the north—and what they lack, I'm certain my friends will bring around when they visit. I do recall the quaint village there. It's a nice ride or walk from the house. They've even got a milliner on their main street."

"A milliner? Oh, how posh," Anise teased with a little laugh.

Poppy drew in a deep breath and grasped her mother's

hands, gaze imploring. "Mama, might we ask that the carriage be prepared earlier so we might leave now? I don't want to be here anymore. And I certainly don't want to see Edward or Mary at the dining table at luncheon."

Anise made a disgusted sound. "The very idea of facing them makes me lose my appetite. I'd rather we get started on our adventure."

"Of course. I'd prefer it as well. I'll have the maids rush to finish up the packing. Seems they are nearly done." She fingered the few dresses left in the closet that needed to be wrapped in tissue.

"Nearly, and I've got a mind to help." Poppy turned around and plucked the other gowns left hanging and took them out to the room onto the bed. "Might as well move this along."

Anise followed suit by taking up the few other personal items they had left about the room and tucking them into a trunk while Mama went off to ask about getting a packed meal.

"Things will be better," Anise said, nodding as if she needed to affirm this for herself as she closed the lid of the trunk and clicked the lock in place.

"Yes. They must be. Anything is better than what we've had to endure here." Poppy hoped they would all find healing in the fresh air because, right now, it felt as if she had an elephant sitting on her chest. "And we'll begin anew."

Anise nodded, moving toward the window to look outside. "The country will be restorative."

"Until winter."

She laughed. "Let's not contemplate snow and ice and misery yet, especially not when the sun is shining today. Besides, sometimes winter can be beautiful too."

"I'll remind you of that when you're shivering before the fire and unable to go for your walks for days at a time."

"I'll probably need the reminder, though right now, the idea of being surrounded by a blanket of white with a hot cup of tea does sound romantic and heavenly."

"Until Mama asks you to get more wood for the fire."

"More wood? Why would I do that?" Anise asked.

"We're not likely to have many servants," Poppy mused. "We've got the house and our tiny incomes."

"I hadn't thought of that. Do you remember what the dower house looks like?" Anise wrinkled her nose, a finger pressed to her chin. "I admit to not having the faintest idea."

Poppy tried to think back to when she'd been a girl and they'd visited it one summer. "I think it's rather small. A couple of bedrooms, two or three. A dining room, a drawing room. Kitchen. Servants' quarters."

"So, if there are only two bedrooms, we shall be sharing again?" Anise plucked a painting from the wall, opened the trunk, and stuffed it inside.

"But we shall have plenty of countryside to explore if that's the case. And what are you doing? Don't you think Mary will inspect this entire room?"

Anise grinned. "Oh, my, I can't wait. Either she'll ride down the road on horseback or send a scathing letter to Mama about our thievery. Either way, I shall have a pretty portrait of Edinburgh Castle to hang over the hearth in the drawing room."

"You're wicked, Anise," Poppy teased.

"Mary likes to kick us when we're down. We've got to be able to pay her back somehow."

"It's true. We do."

Poppy and Anise finished packing their rooms, and then,

when it was time to depart, they did so without a backward glance.

The three women climbed into the carriage. No Edward or Mary to wish them well. However, their little boy waved from where he stood beside his governess.

Mama smiled at them inside the carriage. "We'll make it through, my dears. It is the strength of one named Featherstone. Our demeanors may come off light as a feather, but when one gets the heart of it, we are solid as stone."

"But not stony in countenance," Anise added.

"Nor flighty like a feather," Poppy grinned.

"Exactly. We are a conundrum to those who don't understand us, yet they cannot help but admire us." Lady Cullen waved goodbye to no one in particular. "Goodbye, sweet city, for now. This is not the last society has seen or heard from us."

Anise grabbed Poppy's hand. Her fingers were chilled, likely from nerves, just as Poppy's were. They were all making a great show of it. But the truth was, Poppy was scared of what was to come, as much as she was relieved to have the darkness of her sister-in-law's moods behind her.

Poppy grinned at her mother and sister, grateful for their company. They had each other, and that was a treasure in itself. While there was so very much changing in their worlds, at least there were a few things that remained the same.

🐿 10 🐿

Every horse and cart, carriage and pedestrian bounced in front of Dougal as he scrambled back down the street on horseback toward Leven House. Even a dog, a cat and a bird got in his way as if the universe were conspiring against him. Why had it not occurred to him to ask if they'd like his escort before? What an idiot he'd been to leave.

"Confound it," he growled as he finally arrived at what appeared to be a quiet house.

Dougal practically leapt off his horse in his haste, marching up to the front door. He raised his hand, prepared to demand entry, but before he could knock, the butler opened the door and peered out with an expression that said he was too late.

"I'm too late." The words fell from Dougal's mouth, landing like a pile of rocks at his feet.

Grant's expression was grim as he gave a curt nod. "Aye, my lord. They left a half hour ago."

Hell and damnation. Dougal fisted his hands at his sides in frustration, thinking today of all days might be a good one to let off steam in the Duke of Sutherland's gymnasium. Except there was no time for that either. "I thought they were leaving after luncheon?"

Grant nodded once more. "Aye, my lord, but the lasses requested an earlier departure." He leaned in closer, the way he'd started to do now. "To be frank, I think the idea of waiting until luncheon to face their...family, was a bit much."

Dougal couldn't blame them for trying to get out of the house quicker than originally planned. He wouldn't want to remain any longer either. And sitting around waiting for luncheon, where Mary would lord it over them that she was getting her way sounded miserable.

Dougal considered hopping on his horse and riding all the way to the Highlands. Given his message, his servants there would already be aware of his impending arrival. Then he'd ride to the dower cottage in Skerray and... And what?

Invite them to dinner? Invite himself to dinner? Insert himself in their lives?

What right did he have to do that? Poppy would never be his. He wasn't free to give himself to her. Until he dealt with the Lucia situation, there was nothing he should be doing about Poppy.

He should let her go.

Let her live her life without him.

And yet... The urge to chase after her was so strong within him that he had to brace himself on the front stoop of the Leven residence rather than turn toward his mount.

The fact of the matter was that he was fairly certain...he was *in love* with Poppy Featherstone.

"Are you well, my lord?" Grant eyed him with concern, looking ready to grab Dougal if he somehow collapsed.

"Nay," he croaked, every emotion swirling into a tight knot that held his tongue in his throat.

The butler nodded. "Neither am I if I may be so bold. Is there anything I can do for ye, my lord?"

Dougal shook his head, flexing his fingers, which had become numb in his clenched fists. There was nothing to do. At least, nothing anyone else could do. "Good day," Dougal managed to say.

"As well to ye, my lord." Grant nodded, though he didn't close the door, just watched him with that same look of concern.

How terrible did he look on the outside that the butler seemed ready to catch him?

Dougal cleared his throat and turned around, taking the steps a bit slower than usual in case his body decided to plant him on the ground in retaliation for this situation being so out of control.

As Dougal rode back down the street toward his house, a familiar carriage sat out front. The crest of Lucia Steventon's father was boldly gilded on the side.

She'd returned. *Bloody fecking hell.* This was the last thing he needed. The absolute last. Of all the blasted timing!

His insides hardened as if he'd swallowed a boulder molded by his sister. Lucia opened the window of her carriage as he passed. She popped out her pretty blonde head and smiled at him as if she'd finally found the treasure she'd been searching for.

Dougal couldn't help his surprise and attempted to mold his expression to say otherwise. This was highly improper. Ladies did not arrive at men's homes, even if they were engaged. Even if her presence was desired—though, in this case, it was not.

"My lord." Lucia's tone was familiar, even though she used a formal expression. Her gaze roved over his figure on the horse. "I was hoping to catch you. It's been so long since we last saw each other."

Dougal made a noncommittal noise in the back of his throat, uncertain what to say in this particular situation. A polite gentleman might invite her inside, but a polite gentleman would also be worried about inviting her inside. And while he was mostly polite, he wasn't feeling very courteous at the moment, considering Lucia had decided to come back from a decade abroad to nail the lid on his coffin.

"We were passing by," she continued, waving her hand inside the carriage to someone he couldn't see.

At that moment, the carriage door opened on the other side. But the person stepped around the back to greet him. Sir George Steventon.

Dougal held his grimace tightly inside, not wanting the elder gentleman to see his displeasure at such a visit. It was one thing for a lady to come uninvited to a man's house, quite another for her to show up with her father.

"I inquired inside, but you weren't here." The statement sounded almost like an accusation. The man was gray all over his head, thinning at the temples, and had a permanently pinched look about his face. No doubt, with a daughter like Lucia, he was kept plenty on his toes.

Dougal managed to clear his throat, hoping it would clear his head and give him the right thing to say, but alas, no luck.

Dougal dismounted, holding the reins and keeping his horse between him and the carriage. Fortunately, he was tall enough to see well over the animal, though Sir George had to look up. Poor fellow.

"Do come in, then." Though the invitation was given, it wasn't given with pleasure. Dougal didn't feel the need to be friendly. After all, they were putting him out, and he might as well set a tone now. The last thing he wanted to do was invite them inside to be browbeaten into a marriage he'd forgotten about. And one that seemed suspiciously convenient now for a woman he'd not seen in years. If only he could crack open their heads like a couple of walnuts and figure out what had brought them here.

Once settled in his drawing room, Dougal called for tea. He sat opposite the father and daughter. Lucia looked even more boring than she had before. Her face was expressionless. Her eyes lacked life. How had he once found her captivating? His gaze fell on the sideboard where a crystal decanter gleamed in the sunlight, beckoning him to drink the contents. That was how, of course. Drink seemed to give a man a different view of people, women in particular.

"Glad we caught you in town," her father said, shifting on his chair. The way his gaze wouldn't quite meet Dougal's rankled.

"Very lucky indeed, as I am leaving shortly," Douglas said, making the declaration before he'd even had a chance to contemplate if that were what he would be doing.

The only plans he'd made thus far were to open his castle in the north. But they need not know another thing about it. Only that he was unavailable for whatever *this* was. Felt like an ambush, to be sure.

"Is that so?" Lucia's father seemed perturbed, glancing at his daughter, who wore an equally perturbed expression, but Dougal didn't care. "We were hoping to get a wedding date established."

Now was the chance for Dougal to call off the whole thing, but he didn't want to embarrass Lucia nor incite her father into calling him out into a duel. But he also couldn't ignore the reminder of a life they hadn't planned. A foolish whim they'd shared a decade ago when both of them had been practically children and both in their cups. This matter needed to be settled before it went any further.

"I dinna believe a formal proposal has been made," Dougal countered. He kept his expression neutral, daring them to argue.

Lucia sat up straighter and, to her credit, made her expressionless face form into embarrassment—for him. She even blushed a little. Och, but she was cunning. "My lord, you have forgotten. Friends surrounded us. Many witnesses to your declarations of...love." At this, her hand fluttered to her heart, and she batted her lashes.

He'd seen better acting at Covent Gardens. She was truly bad at this, and she clearly wanted something from him. Needed something.

Sir George sputtered, hands pressed to the arms of his chair, knuckles going white. What exactly had she told her father? For Dougal was certain she'd told him a tall tale.

Dougal remembered that night, though not very well. The rounds and rounds of ale. The drams and drams of whisky. How his friends, including Colonel Austen, had hoisted them on their shoulders. How Lucia wasn't supposed to be out. How she and several of her friends had somehow managed it, meeting up with the lot of them at someone's house. A friend he couldn't even remember now. The scandal that should have gone in the paper but didn't because they'd all kept quiet about it.

"Is it not your birthday in a fortnight?" Lucia asked shyly. "I've never forgotten."

Dougal felt as though he'd slipped into a nightmare that he couldn't get out of. This was ridiculous. He wanted to shout, "If ye'd not forgotten, then where have ye been? What is going on right now that has made ye come back?"

"I do believe there's been a misunderstanding." Dougal was quite proud of the way he kept his tone even.

Did Lucia believe him such a gentleman that he wouldn't rat her out for her debauchery?

"I don't believe there's been anything of the sort," Sir George said, and Dougal felt bad for the man being so thoroughly duped by his daughter.

The right thing to do would be for Lucia to tell her father. Which did not appear to be something she was interested in doing.

Dougal looked at her pointedly, encouraging without words for her to come clean. But the stubborn chit raised her chin and gave him a look that he'd seen a hundred times on Mary's face. She was digging in her heels, and she was going to make him pay if he so much as tried to change her plans.

Fabulous, he thought with all the sarcasm he imagined Poppy would say.

"You had an agreement to wed on your twenty-ninth birthday," Sir George continued as if Dougal had agreed. "Now, given it is in a fortnight, I'm not certain that we'll be able to make that date, but we can get close if we begin planning now and announce the banns."

Lucia nodded and glanced at her father with a treacle-sweet smile, then back to Dougal, her expression cooling. "Your sister has very kindly offered to help. And I'm so glad she contacted me when she did to let me know you were finally ready for me to come back to London and begin a life with you. I do hope you've enjoyed these past years and the special gift of time I gave you."

Dougal almost spit out his tea, but rather than the tea spewing from his mouth, he sucked it back in, choking on the leafy water. He started to cough, hoping that maybe the tea would take him out now. Dying seemed preferential to whatever this madness was.

Neither of his guests offered assistance. Lucia looked put out that he would cough over what she'd said, and her father looked at Dougal as though he were a toddler throwing a tantrum. The both of them were horrid people, he decided. Absolutely horrid.

Horrible people often made friends with one another, which explained Lucia and Mary's connection.

Of course, his sister was behind this. And contrary to what Lucia had said, Mary had never done anything kind a day in her life. But that also answered a burning question he'd had for days: who had orchestrated all of this? Lucia, though clever and devious as she'd proven, still didn't strike Dougal as a mastermind.

Mary, on the other hand, was a schemer to a fault and constantly looking for ways to ruin his and everyone else's lives. He wouldn't doubt that she'd kept a note in her diary to send Lucia a reminder of their promise and ticked off the days over the last ten years until she could make that happen. But perhaps his obvious interest in Poppy Featherstone had been the straw that broke the camel's back. For whatever reason, Mary could not abide the two of them being happy together.

"Are you an honorable man, Lord Reay?" Sir George asked, his yellowing teeth showing in what might pass for a smile if he were a monster hiding under the bed.

Dougal gritted his teeth. "Of course, I am." For the man to suggest otherwise was a great insult, and in his own home no less.

"Then I do not think we have anything else to discuss other than the marriage settlements. I've taken the liberty of having my solicitor draw up an appropriate contract, sir."

He reached into his coat, pulling out a thick packet of papers.

Dougal cleared his throat, grateful for a wee reprieve as he tried to buy a few minutes to think about this. He would certainly not sign the stack Sir George held, and he also couldn't agree to look it over. He wouldn't go to his desk, pull out paper and take notes on terms to send to his solicitor. That would only give credence to this insane situation. When a man and woman married, they should both want it. And it wasn't as if he'd gotten Lucia with child and was honor-bound to marry her. Hell, he hadn't even kissed her. Though he'd watched her kiss plenty of the other lads that night.

If every man who declared his love for a woman while in a drunken haze was then reduced to marrying her, the world would be a very wedded place. And to be fair, he'd only once told Lucia he loved her.

He glanced down at her midsection now, wondering if she'd gotten into a bad way with someone abroad. If the result of that union had forced her to seek him out, Mary's letter had come to her at a most fortuitous time. Was she trying to pawn a bastard off on him?

Lucia glared at him when he met her gaze, but nothing in her angry expression gave away the truth. He'd only be able to find that out when she started to round and then only for certain when she gave birth. And he'd have to stay away from her, never lay with her, just as proof. But by then, they'd already be wed, this farce complete, and nothing he could do about it.

There was always an annulment. But what was the use of even putting himself into a situation like that? It would be stupid.

Time for him to put an end to his meeting.

"I dinna discuss anything without my solicitor, nor do I

look over terms without him," Dougal said. "And he is currently out of town. I will send him a note to be in touch with me upon his return, and then we will contact ye in regard to this matter."

Lucia scowled at his terminology, but Dougal didn't want to put voice to anything close to betrothal that could be construed as consent to the agreement.

Besides, Mr. Cole, his solicitor, was not out of town. Dougal would be certain to have a meeting with him as soon as he could get these two out of his hair.

"I do hope you understand the seriousness of this situation," Sir George said, speaking to Dougal as if he were a child in need of education.

He'd had enough. Politeness didn't seem to be the appropriate way to respond now, and it certainly hadn't gotten him anywhere in the last few days since he'd found out that Lucia was coming to make good on a flimsy comment at best.

"I hardly think using the word 'serious' in conjunction with a drunken nineteen-year-old's ramblings is appropriate, sir, and yet here we are. I have some business to attend to, so while this meeting has been...interesting, I'm afraid I'll have to ask ye to depart."

The older man bared his teeth, smacking his lips together the way Dougal had seen a rabid dog do once. Lucia, too, started to hem and haw. Before either of them could say something that they'd regret, Dougal stood.

"I'll remind ye that ye came by unannounced. And if I were I no' a generous man, I might have denied ye entry merely on the rudeness of such an act, and by society's mark, I'd have been within my rights to do so. I am, however, gracious when needed."

Lucia stood, understanding that Dougal was annoyed and quite serious, before her father did. She also seemed to understand that if she were to get what she wanted, she needed to behave—not that Dougal had any plans to give her what she wanted.

"Come along, Papa, we needn't take up any more of my *fiancé's* time." When she said fiancé, she looked hard at Dougal. "Besides, I need to get ready for tea at my dear friend Lady Leven's. I quite look forward to getting to know my future sister-in-law better."

Dougal kept his smile placid, not interested in engaging in whatever mind game she was attempting to start. He'd said his piece, and he intended to find a way out of this and to get to the bottom of her sudden interest in him.

"Oh, by the way," Lucia said as she neared the door to the drawing room, "Lord Campbell sends his regards and congratulations to the two of us."

Dougal turned his back to hide his bristle. Campbell had been present during the unfortunate evening Dougal had drunk too many whiskeys and then made the most idiotic declaration of his life. Campbell also hated Dougal for beating him out of several honors at Oxford and warning Mary against him. The man didn't understand Dougal was doing him a favor, for he'd not wish his sister on anyone.

How interesting that he was still in touch with Lucia. Again, he glanced toward her midsection, wondering if it was Campbell who might have planted his seed there. The web of who was involved with the reminder of this ridiculous proposal grew wider.

One week later

The countryside was lovely. That wasn't a lie.

Nor was it a lie to say that the village of Skerray was quaint.

The house was also quaint.

But when Poppy told herself that she could be happy living in the country in the quaint village in the quaint cottage, she was lying. And it wasn't because any of those things in particular, or even put together, made her unhappy. It was merely the circumstances that had brought her here and the uncertainty of a future none of them had planned.

And the fact that it did not appear anyone had kept up with the cottage since she'd visited as a child.

Several shutters were hanging off the hinges, and the door looked as old as William the Conqueror. Creeping vines had rooted their way up the sides of the house, which could be pretty, but so many of the vines' leaves had browned and grown tangled that it looked messy rather than magical.

The yard was overgrown, too, and while it looked as if someone had attempted to hack at the overgrowth to create a path, they had given up.

"Oh, my," Mama said. "Perhaps inside will look better."

Poppy and Anise exchanged a look. The servants had been sent ahead of them to prepare, but they might have had only a day or two in advance, given the time of their departure, and from the looks of it, they needed a whole month to get it into working order.

As the carriage came to a stop, several people rushed from the house to make a line. Their clothes were dust-covered as they'd already been working hard to prepare the place.

"This will be an adventure," Poppy said. "We just have to remember that, and who doesn't love an adventure?"

Anise and her mother gave her skeptical looks, and then the three of them bustled out of the carriage.

They were introduced to their small staff—a housekeeper/cook, a scullion/maid, and a lady's maid for the three women to share. A man would also work as a groomsman, butler and gardener, calling himself a Jack of all trades.

And that was it.

The servants themselves were a family. Mother and father and their two children, who all lived in a small house a little bit away from the property, meaning that at night, when the lights were doused and all were abed, the house would be empty, except for Poppy, Anise and their mother. She'd never slept in a house without servants. And the idea of doing so was rather unnerving.

Who would protect them should something go awry?

What if they needed something? Were hungry?

The realization had not hit her before. How very spoiled she was, not even used to making her tea.

This was an awakening for certain. Did she even know how to make tea?

They moved into the cottage, where their new house-keeper, Mrs. Bromley, gave them a nice tour, showing them their rooms, and at Poppy's request, instructed her on how to make tea.

Though the outside had looked less than promising, the truth was that the staff had done an excellent job of cleaning up the inside. The surfaces were dusted, the rugs beaten, and the windows opened to let in fresh air. The kitchen was spotless, and the servants had even stocked them with provisions. The bed sheets were clean and smelled like the Highlands air, and the drawing room had a shelf of books that Poppy was dying to read.

By nightfall, she was feeling better than when they'd first arrived. There were three bedrooms as well, so she and Anise were not forced to share, though that first night, they did anyway because they'd never slept alone in a house without at least one servant there. Safety in numbers wasn't something she'd thought about until now.

She had spotted a fire poker in her bedroom that she could use for protection, which she kept close by when they blew out the candles at night. But the thing was so heavy she wasn't certain she'd be able to grab it and make good use of it. Besides, keeping it under her pillow had left ashes on her sheets, making her immeasurably guilt-ridden when Elizabeth, their upstairs maid, saw it the next morning. Guilt had made her ask to help with chores, which she found satisfying, as odd as that might seem. She was accomplishing something, even if it was beating out her frustration on a rug.

But she needed something to keep her safe. It was just the

three of them, and word traveled fast, especially in small villages. All would know it was only the three of them—the honorable and the not-so-honorable. This meant that if someone had less than honorable designs, they could enter the premises with a few good tricks and commit their crimes with ease.

It was because of this realization manifesting into a nightly fear that three days after they'd moved into the cottage, Poppy went into the small village general store and bought a hammer, which she kept under her side of the bed should she need to defend her family.

For three mornings in a row, she'd found the hammer missing, and each time, she found it in the tool shed.

"Elizabeth, why do you keep taking my hammer?"

Elizabeth's face paled, and she looked toward the ground. "I put it back where it belongs."

"It belongs where I left it under my pillow."

"Yes, my lady," she said, though her expression begged to know why.

"Please do not remove it." Poppy kept her gaze steady and decided to be open with her maid. "It is quite dark here at night, and we are quite alone."

Elizabeth's mouth popped open as if she had only now comprehended. "I understand, my lady."

Later that afternoon, after coming back from a long walk with Anise, Poppy found not only new locks on the front and back doors of the house but in the bedrooms as well—and her hammer where it was supposed to be, under her pillow.

"Poppy," Anise's voice was filled with excitement as she burst into Poppy's bedroom, waving a piece of paper. "We've been invited to a dance."

Poppy put down the brush she'd been using to brush her hair as Elizabeth was assisting her mother with her morning bath. And besides, she could brush her hair. A simple braid was all she needed in the country. No intricate hair styles here.

"A dance?" After being in the Highlands for two weeks, she hadn't been sure dances were part of the culture this far north of Edinburgh, even if Dougal and her brother had assured her society was alive and well in these parts. To her, they could have been dumped in the middle of nowhere.

"Aye, look." Anise thrust the invitation toward her. The paper was simple, and the calligraphy was simpler. As simple as the house and as quaint as the village. Where she was at first disparaging, she now found it charming.

The dance was to be held at a dance hall—which Poppy hadn't realized this small town had. A bonus. Where could it be? She'd not seen one near the general store or the milliners.

"Say you'll go with me," Anise begged, going so far as to get down on her knees and put her hands together in prayer.

"Oh, do get up, sister. We beat these rugs often, but you're wearing white, and even a clean rug isn't fully clean when it comes into contact with white. Of course, I'll go."

Anise leapt to her feet and wrapped her arms around Poppy. "Thank you so much, Poppy. You have no idea what this means to me. Let us see what we can wear, and maybe we can convince Mother to take us into town for some new ribbons for our hair at least."

"I think we can manage a few new ribbons for certain. It's not as if we're asking for new Highland trousseaus."

Anise clapped excitedly and danced around the room with a pretend partner.

"Is it too much to hope that Sir John will come? He did promise."

"If he promised, then I suspect he will." Poppy sat back against her chair, her brush forgotten as she watched her sister, living vicariously through her happiness. She chose not to think of how unlikely it was for a young, handsome and wealthy man like Sir John to leave a city full of other eligible brides and ones with significantly higher dowries.

As it turned out, they needn't have convinced Mama about the ribbons, for as soon as their mother found out there was to be a dance, she declared it a village shopping day and ordered the curricle readied. The dower cottage had an old curricle that Jack had fixed for them. The carriage they'd had for the long ride from London had already been returned to her brother's residence, though he'd been charitable enough to provide them with two horses.

"I prefer to walk into town," Poppy said as her mother and Anise prepared to climb into the curricle with Anise grabbing hold of the reins. "The two of you go ahead of me."

"Are you afraid of my driving skills?" Anise asked suspiciously.

Poppy laughed. "No, but now that you point it out."

"Oh, you," Anise scoffed, but her eyes glinted.

"I merely thought the air would do me good and that as soon as you saw the modiste's shop, you'd be looking for a ready-made dress, too, and I've plenty of gowns to keep me satisfied."

Anise's face lit up. "A lovely idea to look for dresses! I shall dine on bread the rest of the month. Perhaps we should have a few made."

"Perhaps just one," Mama said, at least seeing some sense. "But I don't like the idea of you walking, dear."

"A walk will do me some good, Mama, I promise. And it's perfectly safe."

"Shall I walk with you?" Anise said. The two of them did enjoy their walks together. "Mama can handle the reins, can you not, Mama?"

"I have been known to handle a horse or two in my day."

Poppy shook her head. "Not this time. Don't worry so much. Go on into town. I'll see you all soon."

Poppy laced her boots up and started on her walk. They weren't far from the village. Perhaps a mile or so. The sky was blue, the sun high, and she tied on a bonnet to keep herself from getting a sunburn.

The exercise felt amazing, but she needed the quiet time to think more. With the house so small, she never felt she had any time to herself. And she so loved to think and ponder. To contemplate what they were going to do with their lives. She might need to start incorporating a daily walk. She had spent most of her time helping their sparse staff keep the household running so that Mama and Anise could relax and be happy. Their nerves were much more delicate than hers.

But until this moment—when she was outside in the sun, stretching her legs, feeling the invigoration of movement—she had not realized how much she'd missed and needed this.

She sauntered down the road, looking at the swells of the hills and moors, the various houses and cottages that dotted the landscape. The sheep and cattle. She plucked a flower from where it grew between the two stones that made up the wall beside the road, also serving as a fence on someone's property to keep their animals from wandering.

It was a tiny white flower, its petals delicate as she stroked them. She tucked it near her ear, between the ribbon and her bonnet for an added feminine touch.

She was excited about the dance, curious about what it might be like given the difference in landscape. Would their dances be the same? The punch? Would their evening gowns be out of place? Did people in the county wear gowns? Or did they don their best day dresses?

Poppy wasn't ready to go to a dance yet, but their situation was one she felt partially responsible for. Perhaps if she'd been nicer to Mary, there might not have been a rivalry. But even as she thought it, she knew it for the rubbish it was. Dougal was right about one thing, even if he was a heart-breaker—his sister lived to torment others.

And so, Poppy was going to go and make the best of their new life. The Highlands were truly stunning. She was lucky to live in such a gorgeous and peaceful place, truly.

At the dance, she'd perhaps try to make some friends, in addition to meeting a few eligible bachelors she might be able to add to a list she'd started in her diary, which was still blank. Only the title stood out on the top of the page: *Potential Husbands*.

The one name she would have liked to add there was one she never would. The notebook had been a gift from her father, and she'd never known what to write in it. Potential husbands seemed like a good entry. And yet that too was blank, just like the rest of her future. It was a wide-open canvas ready to be filled.

Somehow, she had to erase Dougal from her mind. And the only way to do that was to put herself back on the marriage market.

Miss Poppy Featherstone—an accomplished woman nearing spinsterhood—do we have any bidders?

She sighed, seeing her thoughts turning melancholy, and determined she needed to push past those dour contemplations and focus on the good. The things she was grateful for.

The rest of her walk into town flew by as she admired the atmosphere and landscape of Skerray. Took in the sea-salt scent of the coast. And when she made it into the small village, she smiled at its quaintness rather than frowning.

Mama and Anise were coming out of the drapers, spotting her right away.

"Did you find a dress?" Poppy asked.

"A lovely one in a dusky rose. She took my measurements to take it in, but thinks it will be ready in time." Anise's smile was contagious.

"How lovely."

There were new ribbons and a new pair of slippers each, though Poppy did try to dissuade her on the last bit. Each pair of slippers costs as much as nearly a fortnight's supply of food. But Mama wouldn't hear of it and said she'd be happy to dine on bread the rest of the season if it kept her girls in good slippers. Poppy did not think it was likely to come to that, but nevertheless was determined to find a book in the house on gardening in case she needed to start planting their own food.

12

Dougal had always believed himself to be a man of action.

When a tenant on one of his properties was in need, he would roll up his sleeves and help out however he could. Whether it was herding sheep, mending a fence, or climbing a roof to put on new thatch.

If one of his friends called in a favor, Dougal saw it done, only stopping short of murder—not that anyone had yet to ask.

Even for his seat in Parliament, he signed the requisite documents, listened to the ridiculous speeches, and made his own opinions and initiatives known. He stood up for what was right and fought for the people rather than those who wished to make themselves richer.

This particular situation with Lucia Steventon was no different.

And since when did he let himself be strong-armed into a situation he couldn't get out of? He was a grown man. An educated and intelligent man. A man of action.

Not some idiotic adolescent with half a brain.

Lucia and her father were not going to force him into a marriage. Especially not a marriage that shouldn't be happening. But he was concerned about Campbell. Dougal had sent out an investigator who found out that Campbell had been abroad and crossed paths with Lucia many times. Having been one of the witnesses a decade ago to his declaration, it made sense that Campbell would attempt to "steal" Lucia from him or, at the very least, make a cuckold of Dougal.

And so, he climbed onto his horse and rode to Aberdeen to see his Aunt Judith, a trip that took several days. But rather than arriving weary, he'd had nearly eighty hours to ponder and plan.

Now, as he sat before her at tea, she stared down her long nose at him, all the judgment of the world in her aging eyes.

"What do you mean it wasn't a real engagement?" she asked.

Dougal recalled a particular time in his youth when he'd lost a horse. Went out riding and then hopped off to chase a frog. The horse disappeared for three days. His aunt had given him the same look back then and asked nearly the same question: "What do you mean you lost a horse?"

Whether he was eight or twenty-eight, Judith had the power to make him feel like a young lad.

"I never proposed, Aunt. I merely suggested while in a drunken state that if I wasna married by my twenty-ninth birthday, she and I should wed." He didn't want to tell her about Campbell because he had no proof that his suspicions were true. Aye, they'd spent time together abroad, but that didn't mean they'd climbed into bed together.

Aunt Judith pursed her lips, her teacup suspended in mid-air. She placed it carefully back on the saucer and stared at him with narrowed eyes for so long he wasn't sure if she'd fallen asleep or had somehow magically been able to conjure his memories to see for herself.

"You aren't twenty-nine yet," she said at last.

Dougal's mouth went dry at what he thought she might be implying. Not yet twenty-nine meant he didn't have to follow through.

"Do you need me to explain it to you plainly?" Aunt Judith cocked her head as if she were asking if he needed help washing his hands. A minor task that was self-explanatory, but perhaps he hadn't the mental capacity to see it done.

Humoring her, Dougal nodded and picked up his tea.

Aunt Judith cleared her throat and straightened her spine, somehow able to look down on him from her tiny stature. "If that was the stipulation, and you don't wish to see it through, then the only other alternative, as I see it, is to find someone else who will marry you in the next two weeks before your birthday comes around."

Now, that was not what he'd thought, and so perhaps his hand-washing analogy only made him seem dense. Marry someone else? Like bloody hell he would. Unless it were Poppy. But she...

"Impossible," he grumbled, sticking his tea back on the saucer and grabbing a raspberry biscuit to shove into his mouth to keep himself from saying another word.

Judith frowned—well, perhaps she frowned harder. "How so? You're a handsome and wealthy earl. What young lady wouldn't want to be a countess? I suspect if I were to go into Edinburgh now and simply stand in the square and shout out the details of your fortune, there would be hundreds, if not thousands, of women lining up. There might be more who'd take their carriages up from London to stand before you and declare themselves the winner of your affections. Shall I ring for my carriage?"

Dougal shook his head, feeling the need to stretch but being held prisoner in this chair. "That would be no different than marrying Lucia Steventon."

Aunt Judith returned to her quizzical inspection. "If that's the case, then what is the problem?"

"I dinna want to marry her." He was aware that he sounded like a petulant child, but Dougal believed marriage was not just a financial transaction or a contract signed. He believed that if he were going to align himself with a woman for the rest of his life, she'd better be someone he wanted to wake up beside every morning and do so with a smile. A woman whose company he enjoyed, who had similar habits, and who enjoyed similar activities.

"Do you want to marry someone else in particular?"

Dougal gritted his teeth to keep his mouth from falling open at being so obvious. "I want to have control over my fate."

His aunt laughed. "A worthy ambition, save for the fact of your birth. You were born into the aristocracy. You haven't been able to choose what you could do with your life from the moment you took your first breath. Control over one's life is only an illusion, especially for a lad in your position."

"I think I should be offended."

She shrugged. "Take offense to the facts if you like. That will do little good for your situation. Nothing changes."

"What if there were a lady I was interested in?" Poppy's face flashed before his mind, smiling, eating her iced cream—but the image blurred and then he saw her glaring at him from across a drawing room.

"Then I suggest you get in touch with her as soon as possible and see if she'd be willing to say 'I do' with you before the time is up."

Dougal grimaced.

"What is it?" Aunt Judith's tone was impatient. "Might as well tell me, as we've already crossed the lines of propriety by discussing how to thwart your current fiancée."

"She's no' my fiancée."

"Only according to you."

Dougal felt like stomping his foot and groaning and shouting as he might have had he still been a lad—he was starting to feel much like one.

"There is a lady I've been acquainted with for some years. I had hoped to...to ask her to be my wife at some point, but I wanted to woo her more. She can be quite hard to read sometimes. And well, at the moment, she rather dislikes me."

"Does she need to like you to say yes?"

Dougal gave an exasperated expression.

"Ah, you do not know if she'd accept."

"Aye. Sometimes, I'm not certain she even likes me. And in the current hour, I'm certain she hates me."

"Why is that?"

"Because she knows about Lucia Steventon and believes I was using her for my own entertainment."

Aunt Judith gasped, her hand fluttering to her wrinkled neck. "You didn't, Dougal. Shame! I ought to have you whipped."

He frowned for half a second until he realized what she thought he was implying. "Oh, for shame, Auntie, no' that. I merely flirted. A kiss or two."

"A kiss to a woman is all but a declaration of love," she said, her cheeks flaming, and she whipped open a fan to cool herself—either that or to shoo him away. "Unless she is a doxy."

"Miss Featherstone is no doxy."

Now, it was Aunt Judith's turn to frown once more. "Poppy Featherstone? As in Mary's husband's sister?"

Dougal let out a long, affected sigh. The news was bound to come out at some point. Might as well be now without Mary hovering nearby to box his ears or plan some other form of revenge. "Aye, the verra one."

"Oh, dear me, Dougal. You've really stepped in it." Aunt Judith leaned back in her chair as if he might have a plague and she feared catching it.

"I have. And I think Mary is using my affections for Poppy to punish them."

"She has always been a jealous sort."

"It makes no sense."

"She wants to be the most important lady in Edward's life."

"She is the most important lady in Edward's life. She's his wife."

"Aye, but a mother and sisters can sometimes get under a man's skin."

Dougal laughed. "No' likely with that one. Mary has got herself wrapped around him like a lethal snake. And before you admonish me for saying such about my sister, I do apologize for being unkind."

"Think nothing of it. Whatever is said here will not leave the room. Besides, that might be true concerning Edward, but Mary doesn't always think that far ahead. To her, three women invaded her domain."

"She's getting worse."

"I always thought once she had a son, she would calm down, but it only seems to have made her madder." Aunt Judith shook her head and let out a sad sigh.

"What do I do, Auntie?"

"Oh, pish, darling, it's obvious. Go and try to woo Poppy Featherstone. Be honest with her about what happened with Miss Steventon, and be honest about your intentions and your past transgressions. She, as I recall, is quite an intelligent creature. If she's worth her salt, she'll accept your groveling and say yes."

"She is verra intelligent, which is why she may no' accept."

"She will be hard to win over if she thinks you've betrayed her," Aunt Judith said. "But when have you ever been one to quit?"

Dougal nodded. Winning Poppy over was going to be very difficult indeed, especially after their last meeting when she looked at him as if he were a pile of rubbish—worse than a pile of a rubbish, a pile of rubbish that couldn't stop flinging itself on her. It had gutted him.

But his aunt was right. And Poppy was who he truly wanted to marry. Why wasn't he already there groveling to make it work?

"What are you waiting for?" Auntie stood up, shooing him with her hands. "You only have two weeks, lad. Why waste it here ruminating?"

Dougal leapt to his feet. "Any advice for wooing a lass who hates ye?"

Aunt Judith smiled. "As I said, be honest. She's smart and will see right through any shite you try to feed her."

Dougal blanched. Did his Aunt, the duchess, use an expletive?

"I said what I said." And with her nose up in the air, Aunt Judith marched out of her drawing room, leaving Dougal with his jaw near the floor.

13

The small village was alive after dark, which Poppy found fascinating.

Oil streetlamps crackled and flickered, not yet replaced with gas as they had been in London and Edinburgh. Seeing those flames lick behind the glass gave the village a vintage and cozy feel that Poppy hadn't realized she liked until now.

By the time they'd reached the outskirts of the village, a line of horses and carriages slowed the pace as guest after guest arrived at the dance hall on the other side of town. Perhaps the entire county was coming tonight. And perhaps they'd make a few friends.

Poppy loved her sister, but one thing she'd found since they'd come to Skerray was that she was often lonely. Her friends had yet to visit, and she couldn't blame them. It was the height of the season, and what reasonable lass of marriageable age would abandon the prospects of a proposal to visit a displaced friend?

The closer they drew to the dance hall, the louder the music and laughter filtered through the air. Poppy smiled at

Anise, who'd grasped her hand and practically bounced on her rear in her eagerness to get inside for all the fun.

More so than meeting friends, Poppy hoped for the distraction of a new flirtation, though this time, she wouldn't allow herself to fall as hard as she had for Dougal Mackay. And she certainly wouldn't let anyone kiss her until the ink was dry on the paper. She couldn't let her heart be broken again.

Then again, she did need to remind herself that this time around, it was not about love. Or desire. Nay, this husband hunt was about security.

All she needed was a little bit of interest from a decent man. Someone she could respect and vice versa. A marriage deal. A contract. She needed to wipe all notions of love or anything fanciful from her mind. *Get the deed done, Poppy, so Mama and Anise can relax.*

Save her mother and sister. That was her mission.

They alighted from their carriage and entered the low-lit hall; it was warm with all the bodies crushed together. Scents of candle wax, punch, sweat, and...was that livestock? There was a lingering flower scent from the copious bouquets, perhaps to offset the country smell of—she couldn't quite put her finger on it, but it reminded her of a barn.

"Elizabeth told me that when they aren't using the dance hall for dances, they use it to show off livestock," Anise said, pinching her nose.

"That makes sense." This was the country after all. Spaces had to be used.

A group of musicians played lively music, and dancers frolicked in the middle, their moves slightly more boisterous than one might find in Edinburgh and certainly more than in London.

Poppy smiled, having observed that the farther north one

went, the less all the proper rules of London society mattered, and she rather liked that. Society edicts were too constraining. As she tapped her foot, learning the styles of dance by watching, she found a little more weight removed from her shoulders.

Contradictory with Poppy's desire to be less constrained was that Anise needed all the constraining she could get. Even now, she was squealing and pointing out the handsome gentlemen in attendance.

"Oh, he is certainly delicious. Even rivaling my dear Sir John."

The fact that Anise barely knew Sir John and had only seen him face-to-face twice didn't seem to matter to her when it came to holding him close to her heart. Poppy couldn't decide whether Anise was a romantic or she'd gone mad. But to be fair, the gentlemen she had pointed out were rather handsome in a much more rugged way than either of them were used to.

"Don't point," Poppy said, pushing her sister's hand down. "No need to draw negative attention to yourself. We've only just arrived."

"I can't help it." Anise sighed and pressed her hands to her heart. "Just when I thought my life had taken a bleak turn where love would never touch my heart, we come here, and I can see at least five gentlemen that I'd let—"

"Don't say it."

Anise grinned mischievously. "You know me so well."

"A blessing and a curse."

"Girls, I'm going to get some punch and meet some of the other ladies present. Do behave," their mother said, moving toward the punch table and stopping along the way to introduce herself to several of the other matrons in attendance.

"Shall we mingle?" Poppy asked.

"Of course." Anise put her arm around Poppy's, and they meandered through the hall, weaving this way and that, nodding and smiling.

It was too much to hope they might recognize someone, as Poppy had been so young the last time they were in the area, and she didn't think Anise would remember being here at all. And certainly, none of their London or Edinburgh acquaintances were here.

But the strangest thing happened as they were doing their walk about the room. Sir John—of all people—stepped into their path, a smile on his face.

Poppy practically felt Anise's heart leap from her chest.

"Ladies," he said with a low bow.

Anise gasped and tightened her hold on Poppy. "Sir John, what a surprise," she said, though she didn't seem surprised at all, and the only reason she hadn't tossed herself onto the man, Poppy was pretty sure, was because she held her arm tightly to her.

Poppy squinted her eyes at her sister. What kind of a game was she playing here? Had she told him where they'd be? How? Could a letter travel so fast and he come so far?

It had taken them nearly a week to travel from Edinburgh to Skerray. And why would he have just happened to show up... He must have left town shortly after they did. Where was he staying? What were his intentions? A storm of thoughts battered through Poppy's mind, and while Anise shrieked and giggled, Poppy's brows drew closer and closer until she was fairly certain her face resembled a prune.

"I just so happen to have rented one of the manor houses nearby," he drawled.

Was it bad that Poppy found this to be far-fetched? When had she become so skeptical? Sir John seemed perfectly pleasant, and she had no reason to doubt his intentions or words except for how Dougal disliked him. And was she going to take Dougal at his word? He'd lied to her about being betrothed.

Poppy's stomach soured. All she'd wanted to do tonight was meet new people and have a good time, and now she was being reminded of the people and problems they'd left behind.

Sir John continued, speaking exaggeratedly with his arms moving so much that it was as if he were putting on a play. "I couldn't help but come to the dance tonight in hopes of entertainment, and here I've found two familiar and beautiful faces." He winked as if this were a conspiratorial meeting.

"Oh," Anise sighed, pulling out her fan and fluttering it as their mother did.

"What a coincidence," Poppy said, glancing at her sister, trying to figure out what sort of subterfuge was happening here.

"A happy coincidence," Anise said, the picture of innocence, which to Poppy meant exactly the opposite. Somehow, her sister had arranged this.

"May I be the first to add my name to your dance cards?" Sir John asked.

Anise held hers up so fast he'd barely finished his sentence. Poppy watched as he scratched his name down, not once, but twice, onto Anise's card.

"Miss Featherstone?" he asked, his smile genuine and sweet.

Still, she didn't know if she believed it. Anise elbowed her in the ribs when she hesitated.

She nodded and held her empty dance card out, watching the confident scratch of his name fill out the second spot as he'd taken Anise's first. After he finished writing, she worried he might write his name a second time as he'd done to Anise, but thankfully he didn't. Poppy didn't want to dance with him at all, let alone twice. If he were to show her the same favor he showed her sister, then Anise would certainly be put out about it.

The music ended, and there was a brief pause between sets as partners changed, and others went off in search of refreshment.

"Shall we?" Sir John asked Anise, holding his elbow toward her.

Anise grinned, removing her arm from Poppy's to take his, practically skipping off toward the center of the dance floor as they waited for the next set to commence. A lively reel this time.

Poppy watched, standing alone, as her sister was swept about by the handsome and perhaps too charming Sir John. Wallflower was not a term she was used to thinking of herself as, yet it appeared that might be her lot tonight. As she gazed about the room, more females were in attendance than males, and she was a stranger.

"She is so happy," her mother said beside her, handing her a glass of punch.

Poppy had been so focused on counting those in attendance that she hadn't seen or heard her mother approach. "She is."

Lady Cullen squinted toward the dance floor. "Is that Sir John?"

"It is." Poppy was overly curious to see what her mother thought about his arrival in town.

"Oh, what a dear he is to have come up from Edinburgh to see that she was settled." Mama smiled, the look so tender and nostalgic that Poppy couldn't help but wonder if something similar had happened in her past with either of her husbands.

"You think him honorable, Mama?" Poppy tried to keep her tone neutral, not to draw attention to such a question. If her senses were all wrong, there was no need to get her mother nervous over it.

"I do. He seems sweet on her, and she him. And to have traveled all this way?" Mama let out a long sigh. "We might yet have good news this season."

Poppy pretended to smile. Her fabricated cheer had nothing to do with her sister's happiness; she very much wanted that if she could find it. More so, she couldn't shake the feeling that something was off. There weren't any rumors about him, nor did anyone else in the dance hall seem surprised at his presence. But something was causing her to be vigilant. Perhaps he was too eager? And that eagerness lent to not being genuine?

Anise was beautiful; she was sweet. She was fun. But what about her made Sir John come all this way? Was he in love after only seeing her two times?

"Do you know his circumstances?" she asked.

Mama shook her head. "I hadn't the chance to check prior to leaving Edinburgh. But I'll write a few friends to ask."

"He claims to be renting a manor near town. He must have some means."

"Well, that is impressive. He must intend to court your sister."

"I think he does."

"Then we shall be happy for her." Mama patted Poppy's arm. "There will be a beau for you, too, dear. No need to worry over it."

Poppy nodded, tight-lipped. She wasn't worried about not finding a beau. Already several older gentlemen were eyeing her. If she wanted to be engaged to an octogenarian, she likely could be within the hour.

Perhaps that was what she should do. Offer herself up as the last wish to a dying older gentleman. After all, she had told herself this was a contract, not a love match. A means to an end.

But for every one of the elder gentlemen she studied, from the top of their balding heads to the odd bend of their aging knees, she couldn't find the will to ask for an introduction or even show any interest that might have them come forward. She kept finding herself glancing about the dance hall in hopes that Dougal would appear.

Of all the ridiculous notions. Self-flagellation seemed to be a new hobby for her. For what other reason could she possibly have in trying to hurt herself?

Yet she wished that Dougal, too, would be romantic enough to have come up from Edinburgh like Sir John. To rent a house nearby so she might see him often and believe him when he said he had no intention of marrying Lucia Steventon. For him to sweep her off her feet once more. To bend her over his arm and kiss away all the angst and fear since last season. To be number one in his eyes. To be loved, genuinely and wholeheartedly.

But the one thing she wished for most did not appear.

And why would he? She was a fool even to let herself dream. Better to march into the center of the room and start the bidding for her hand. Though truly, she hadn't much to offer a country gentleman. She wasn't wealthy, and while she had become quite good at beating carpets, she was woefully untrained in any other aspects of running a country home.

Poppy was a city girl, and while she'd never thought of herself as uneducated before, taking her away from that environment left her feeling inadequate.

Still, she looked. Still, she scanned the crowd, bidding them to part to reveal her dark-haired, grumpy hero.

Her heart sank further and further as every minute passed with further disappointment. She declined her dance with Sir John, feigning a headache, and went to sit on the side of the hall like a true wallflower. He took their mother instead, who appeared to be having the time of her life being swung around by a handsome young man.

And finally, after just three dances, Poppy was ready to leave. All the excitement and newness she'd felt earlier when they'd been on the road was gone completely, replaced by melancholy and self-pity.

Anise and Mama joined her for a cup of punch, both full of smiles and redness on their cheeks.

"I am not feeling well," Poppy hedged. "I should like to go home."

"You want to leave? Now?" Anise scoffed. "I don't want to leave. I refuse! What do you mean you aren't feeling well? You were fine moments ago."

Poppy tried to smile but felt a true headache coming on now.

"I'll stay with Anise, dear. You can go home," Mama said, patting her hand. "A good rest will do you some good. Send the carriage back once you've been dropped off."

Anise pouted but nodded, more concerned with herself than Poppy, which was fine. Poppy didn't need any company on the ride home. What she needed was to leave. And what she really needed wasn't even in this county.

Poppy left the dance hall and climbed into the carriage as a pair of riders passed. A tingle made the hairs on the back of her neck rise, and she turned around to get a better look at them, but they were gone, almost as if she'd conjured them up herself.

14

"Thanks for inviting me along," Colonel Austen said as they sat at the breakfast table the following morning after arriving at Castle Varrich.

After traveling for days, subsisting on a few things he'd packed that wouldn't spoil on the road and several tavern meals when they'd stopped to rest the horses, Dougal was ready for a nice home-cooked breakfast. His plate was piled high with eggs, bacon, sausage, mushrooms, beans and thick slices of toast covered in melting butter. Austen's plate looked the same.

"I didna think I was the only one to have something at stake here," Dougal said after swallowing a bite of eggs.

Austen smiled as he dumped three cubes of sugar into his tea. "Ye could tell?"

"Half of Edinburgh could tell," Dougal snorted. "The only reason the other half didna notice is because they are children and were no' in attendance."

Colonel Austen chuckled as he stuffed bacon into his

mouth. "All the same, I'm grateful for your hospitality and your cook. My god, I've no' had a meal this good in forever."

"There is nothing like a Highland breakfast. Shall we ride over to the cottage after breakfast?" The cottage, as they'd come to refer to it, housed both the ladies they were very interested in speaking with.

Colonel Austen had developed a soft spot for Anise, which was somewhat surprising given he'd hardened his heart after what had happened to his first fiancée. The poor woman died of what he'd thought had been scarlet fever, but as it turned out, was syphilis—given to her by a rogue of both their acquaintances. A handsome face had duped Austen's fiancée after being plied with a copious amount of whisky. She claimed to have hardly remembered the event, and when she woke in the morning, he was there, and then he was gone. And shortly after, she was ill, but by the time she'd called for a doctor, the disease had weakened her immune system causing her to get another infection causing all sorts of other issues until she...expired.

There one minute, gone the next.

Austen had never recovered. And until Austen had met Anise, Dougal wasn't certain he was going to ever come out of his understandable melancholy.

Colonel Austen shook his head, looking out the window. Dougal could sense he had some apprehension about their morning plans by the way Austen gripped his fork, knuckles turning white.

Austen cleared his throat. "The ladies may have been at the dance hall last night, and we should probably let them sleep a little longer."

Dougal nodded, understanding that this could be the case and that Austen needed a little time to work himself up to the task and the fear that he might be rejected. Anise had seemed to favor the attention of Sir John, which Dougal found not just irritating but infuriating. If only they knew the depravity of that man. Yet, the colonel, his good friend, had begged him years ago not to say anything about Sir John, and so Dougal had thus far kept his mouth shut. However, he swore that if it looked as if Anise was succumbing to Sir John's charms, he'd have no choice but to share what he knew for the young lass's safety.

"Aye," Dougal said. "Sweet Mary used to sleep all day after a dance."

Austen stopped strangling his fork, letting it fall to the side of his plate. "Perhaps a calling card left with the servants before luncheon would be a good idea? Then they can let us know if they would appreciate our dropping by."

My god, but the man was positively losing his edge. Dougal cocked a challenging brow. "Or we stop by mid-afternoon? Bring them biscuits to go with their tea?"

Austen blew out a heavy sigh that lifted the hair from his forehead. "Why is it so hard to figure out?"

"It really is no', my friend."

But the truth was Dougal was nervous too. He was afraid that if he left a calling card, Poppy would put it in the fire. He could picture her scrunching up her nose in distaste when she read his name and launching the card into the flames as if it were a plague coming to ravage.

But on the other hand, if he dropped by unannounced, Poppy might slam the door in his face or instruct her servants to do that. Or not come out of her room as she'd done to Mary during teatime. The woman was unpredictable. It was part of the reason he liked her, this unpredictable behavior and the very intelligent and independent streak she had. One could never guess what they would get with Poppy. Blast it all, this, everything, was all so confounding.

One perfectly clear thing was that Dougal had to convince Poppy that he'd not tried to deceive her on purpose. That he admired her. That Lucia was not in his life, and not because he was not honorable, but the opposite. That he'd never agreed to wed her, and she had come back to torment him. Although, that last part was a little dramatic. He'd leave that out.

But after he got done telling her how he felt and what he wanted, he needed to see if she'd be willing to marry him. And in his mind, that was yet another opportunity for her to slam the door in his face. Saints, but he was fecked.

The odds were not currently in his favor. And if he were in Poppy's delicate silk slippers, he'd likely smash the door on any matrimonial ideas as well and then have him tossed out on his idiotic arse.

"How the hell has Campbell gotten involved in all this?" Colonel Austen asked, rather shockingly out of the blue.

"Campbell?"

"Oh, come on, man, ye're no' the only one with his ear to the ground. I heard he was somehow involved or that he and Lucia had a short betrothal abroad before he broke it off."

Dougal tried to hide his surprise that Austen knew so much. "I forgot ye practice fisticuffs with Malcolm Gordon."

Malcolm Gordon offered his private detective services to his good friends, which Dougal was lucky enough to count himself.

Austen grunted. "To be fair, it was no' as if he just told me. He asked me when I last saw Campbell and how I'd met him, all that nonsense. I put two and two together when he seemed interested in what I knew of Miss Steventon."

"Clever. But the truth is, I have no idea how the hell he's involved, though I do have my suspicions, and they are all less than honorable. I did ask my solicitor and Malcolm to try and find out as much as possible."

"Campbell was always a scrappy fellow. And a good liar."

"Aye. Remember how jealous he was at Eton and Oxford?" Dougal shook his head. "Doubtful that the man will simply admit that he's held a vendetta against me after plotting out his revenge for a decade and with it coming to a head days before my birthday. That would be mad."

Austen speared a sausage. "He did always strike me as being a little mad, though. Never trusted him. No' even with the simplest things."

"Fair enough." Dougal scooped a large bite of egg onto his fork, devouring his breakfast the same way he always had as a youthful lad full of energy and afraid his schoolmates might come along and take his portion. "I didna either. And I still dinna, and I have no idea what the bloody hell is going on."

"I've made a decision."

"Aye?"

"We'll drop in this afternoon. And after breakfast, we're going to do manly things that make us feel better." Austen said this with a chuckle that Dougal matched.

They spent the morning hunting and riding, and by the time they'd scarfed down a luncheon of sandwiches, Dougal's skin was practically itching to get to the cottage and spill his guts to Poppy. Beg for her on his knees if he must.

"Let's go," Colonel suggested. "Ye're driving me batty with your hand clenching, and your pacing."

"Aye, likewise. Let's get it over with before both of us lose our minds. I will at least know I have no chance and put myself out of my quandary and misery."

"And I shall find out whether that rogue Sir John has made a fool of me and a victim of another woman I care about." There was a heaviness to both their statements that they tried to hide with jovial laughter.

The ride to the small dower cottage was pleasant enough, though Dougal barely noticed, as he practiced what he would say over and over again to Poppy when he knocked on her door. He tried a few lines on Austen, who told him he was well and truly fecked if he didn't get it right.

They had just emerged from a bend in the road with the cottage ahead when a bonneted twosome came into view.

It took Dougal a moment to register who was in front of him, though Colonel Austen thankfully had more sense and urged his horse to stop, and Dougal's horse did the same.

Poppy and Anise.

They were smiling and laughing about something, both practically glowing in the Highland air. He couldn't help but see that Poppy belonged here—that she looked healthier here in the Highlands than the city. Yet when Poppy's gaze met his, there was an infinite sadness that hit him in the gut as though she had taken an axe to his midsection.

She might have looked happy and healthy, but what that look told him was that she was still mad as hell.

"Ladies," Colonel Austen said, sweeping off his hat. "What a fortuitous moment for us to have come upon ye like this."

"Colonel?" Anise said, her mouth forming an adorable *O* of astonishment. "Why, what are you doing so far from the city?" She smiled, but Dougal couldn't help but also sense some distance in her greeting.

Sir John had to be in town. Dougal glanced at Poppy as if to confirm, but her mouth was set in a straight, formidable line. Her expression told him she was not going to give him an inch. For the briefest second, he thought about turning around and going home. Returning to Edinburgh. If he were a lesser man, he might have bowed his head in defeat. But he also knew Edinburgh brought Lucia Steventon and a future far bleaker than getting kicked in the ballocks by Poppy Featherstone. He hadn't set out on this journey thinking it was going to be easy. And in the end if she rejected him, at least he'd given his best effort.

Poppy, even angry and glowering, was the most gorgeous creature Dougal had ever seen. And he longed to see her smile, to see her laughing, to have her give him a witty retort that would keep them bantering for hours.

"Lord Reay." Her voice was as cool as her gaze, and her body language was not at all welcoming. Her rigid spine told him to run the hell away. "What are you doing here?" she asked bluntly.

Honesty—that was what his aunt had said he should use, and it was all that Poppy deserved, so he was honest if not forthcoming. "We came to pay a call."

She wasn't moved. "Why?"

Now, this time, his tongue stiffened. What could he say? He wanted to be honest, but the truth was perhaps too much to toss at her. His truth was something that should probably be eased onto her. A slow reveal. Lord, but he really ought to have planned this better.

"We were in the area." This was true, and he prayed she didn't ask how he happened to be in the area at this precise moment and why he wasn't in Edinburgh, which was several days' ride away. Happening to be in the area was, in truth, quite preposterous.

"Ah, like Sir John. How coincidental that this remote village in the very far north of Scotland happens to be a place people end up in." She cocked her head to the side and offered a smile that was anything but friendly. Then she asked an even worse question. "Where is Miss Steventon? Does she happen to also be in Skerray?"

Colonel Austen cleared his throat, clearly feeling second-hand embarrassment on Dougal's behalf. This was not the first time he'd felt uncomfortable where Dougal and Poppy were concerned. The poor fellow might stop coming on excursions with Dougal if he had to keep witnessing it all. Then again, what were friends for if not to have each other's back? In the battles of war and life, right?

"She is not, I suspect at home with her father." Dougal kept his tone neutral, hoping that would be the end of it, but he could immediately tell it wasn't enough. Saints, but he was mucking this up.

Poppy stuck her nose a little higher in the air. "Oughtn't a man to know where his betrothed is?"

Dougal shrugged, trying for nonchalant, and then he let the truth out for real this time. "I wouldna know the rules for betrothed men, as I am no' one myself."

She rolled her eyes, turned around and marched back toward the cottage. He thought he might have liked it better if she'd told him to fek off.

"I'm afraid you're going to have to do better than that, Lord Reay," Anise said with an expression that said he'd failed miserably.

He nodded, frowning and wishing he'd taken more time to ask his aunt the exact words he should say. "Any advice?"

Anise looked surprised he'd asked, then she licked her lips, going up on her toes and rocking back on her heels, clearly excited. "Poppy needs to feel like she's important. Not because she thinks she deserves it but because of exactly the opposite. Come along, you two. Mama will be glad for some company. And Lord Reay has his work cut out for him."

Anise, too, turned and headed back toward the cottage, the two horsemen following behind.

By the time they arrived at the small cottage, handing their reins to a groom, Poppy was nowhere to be found. But Lady Cullen was beside herself with excitement and ushered them into her drawing room, having already asked tea to be prepared for them.

Dougal glanced up at the ceiling as if he might be able to see through it and ascertain where Poppy was hiding. He had a feeling she wasn't going to come down willingly to speak to him, which was disappointing. How was he to make her feel important if he couldn't find her?

"I've asked for tea, but perhaps you are hungry? Should I have her make some sandwiches? She makes the best little sandwiches. Delicious. We are quite spoiled."

Anise raised her brows and glanced sideways at her mother as if wondering where that had come from and where the mysterious and delicious sandwiches her mother claimed to have were.

"Nay, my lady, we're fine," Dougal said. With them removed to the dower house and having a small income to subsist on, the last thing he was going to do was take their food. "In fact, I've brought ye something that will go well with our tea." He handed her a tin of shortbread biscuits his cook had made for them.

"Oh, you are too kind, Lord Reay. Thank you." She opened the tin and breathed in, her eyes closing as if she hadn't smelled something so delicious in a while.

Anise reached over her mother and plucked one out, biting into it and making a sound of enjoyment. "These are to die for. Mama, have one."

Lady Cullen, too, took a biscuit and delighted in the flavor. Definitely a point in Dougal's favor. He brought good biscuits. He would remember that and bring a tin of biscuits every time.

There was a pause in the room, Lady Cullen and Anise sitting side by side staring, and Colonel Austen looking as if he were about to break out into poetry while he watched the youngest Featherstone.

Dougal glanced back to the door, hoping Poppy was going to walk through. But the door remained closed, and not a sound in the house, not even a creak, gave a hint of where she was hidden. The faintest whisper of her floral perfume was the only sign that she was in residence. Or had been.

"She won't be coming back down," Lady Cullen said, taking note of Dougal's attention. "Headache. So much dancing last night in town. What a wonderful event it was."

There was a twinkle in Lady Cullen's eye that practically said she was lying and hoped he knew it.

15

Poppy stood as still as she could at the top of the stairs, attempting to listen in on the conversation below; however, they weren't talking loud enough. Rather frustrating for those trying to eavesdrop. The other possibility was that she was losing her hearing and was in need of a listening horn, which she didn't have on hand and wasn't likely to find.

Elizabeth came out of Mama's bedroom, having been in there to tidy. She smiled at Poppy and opened her mouth to address her, but Poppy quickly put her finger to her lips. The last thing she needed was for her snooping to be found out by anyone. The house was small. Small enough that at the base of the twelve stairs was the door to the drawing room, and a few feet inside there was Dougal Mackay. She was well and truly only fifteen feet from him.

And it would be mortifying for anyone to realize she was up here snooping.

Especially Dougal, whom she'd given the cut direct on purpose, hoping he would leave, but like a thistle, he'd stuck himself to her metaphorical skirt and come inside.

Elizabeth scooted around her, down the stairs and out of sight. Fortunately, she didn't say anything or give Poppy a look that made her feel sillier than she felt already.

My goodness, the way he'd looked at her when he'd stopped his horse so abruptly. As if he were surprised to see her outside of her own home. As if he hadn't been headed there to see her. And his nonsense about happening to be in the area. There'd been anguish in his gaze when she'd rejected him, and part of her had yearned to stop the hurt.

But she hurt, too, and it had been all his stupid doing.

Why was he even here?

And then he'd claimed not to be betrothed. That Lucia was at home with her father. Did he think that Poppy was stupid? That she would take him at his word? What actually was going on here?

Of course, she knew her questions could be answered if she talked to him instead of eavesdropping.

But she was scared. Because there was a chance he hadn't broken off his engagement, that he was placating her, and that meant he had no business being in her home. Make that no business in Skerray, either. Castle Varrich was at least several miles from the village. That was where he should be, if not back in the city.

To think she'd thought herself special when he had shown up in Edinburgh, had come to her brother's house unannounced, swept into the drawing room, asked her to go for a ride, and then got her iced cream. All of the hopes she'd tried to repress since the previous season when they'd kissed and then he'd abandoned her, had burst through the brick walls she'd built to hold them in, flooding into her with brightly colored fanfare.

Dreams that had been dashed as spectacularly as they'd developed.

Dougal Mackay was too good at breaking down her defenses. Too good for her wellbeing, to be sure. Too much for her to defend herself. She was ready to toss aside her instincts and defenses the moment he was in her presence. Ready to let him lead her down the path of a broken heart again.

She was a fool. And foolish enough to be desperately in love with Dougal Mackay.

Poppy let out a sound of disgust, then clapped her hands over her mouth. Thankfully, at the same time, laughter sounded from the drawing room, a joke she'd missed but had covered up her own noise.

What was he doing in there? Trying to woo her mother over to his side? He would easily transfix Anise, as she was more gullible.

Besides herself, however, Poppy felt the most sorry for Colonel Austen. He'd obviously developed feelings for Anise, and she, in turn, had developed feelings for Sir John, whom she'd danced with not once, not twice, but three times last night. This was a major impropriety on her part, which Mother had allowed in her desperate attempts to find her daughters suitable matches. Tongues were surely wagging this morning about the new lasses on the market and how one had dominated the interest of a handsome, eligible bachelor.

Anise had woken early, expecting to see a note from Sir John, but none had come so far. He'd swept her off her feet and then vanished. Not unlike what Dougal had done to her. Well, hopefully not the same. For her sister's sake, she hoped that Sir John was still in town.

Poppy sank to the top step, her elbows on her knees, her head in her hands.

Below, Elizabeth reappeared and made hand signals that Poppy couldn't identify. Then she motioned as if she were sipping from a teacup, and Poppy decided that must mean she was asking if Poppy wanted to take tea in her room.

No, she didn't want to take tea alone. But neither did she want to take tea in the drawing room with the rest of them.

A quandary. She wanted to know very much what was happening behind closed doors. And very much why Dougal was here and what had happened with Lucia Steventon.

"Shall I pop my head in and get ye a sense of it?" Elizabeth whispered, quite a bit louder than Poppy appreciated.

Poppy's mouth fell open. Had she spoken her thoughts aloud? She was fairly certain she had not, but what she wanted must have been written all over her face. Saints, but she was coming off as desperate and ridiculous.

She shook her head and marched to her bedroom, where she grabbed a book and then took it outside and down the path to a lovely tree she'd found perfect for laying out a blanket and leaning against to read.

The best thing for herself was to extricate herself not only from the reality of Dougal in her house but reality itself. And a book was always the perfect way to do that.

Poppy flipped to where she'd left off, tugging out the bookmark her mother had embroidered for her last Christmas. She read the same paragraph three times, her mind continuously wandering back to the cottage.

"Enough, you silly girl," she said aloud, huffing a breath and starting again.

After several more attempts, she was finally invested enough in the story, but then perhaps not. Her eyes started to droop as if her mind had decided that if she couldn't escape into a book, then she was going to escape into sleep. The idea of going back into the house when their guests were likely still there, as she hadn't seen them leave, was abhorrent. Perhaps a nap here? Would that be considered dangerous?

Likely not. And so, she let her eyes fall closed, her book laid beside her, the bookmark back in place to mark the page.

"Miss Featherstone?"

A second later, nay, it must have been longer for the sun had started to set, Poppy's eyes flew open to find Dougal peering down at her.

"Your mother and sister will be glad to know ye've no' been abducted." His grin was teasing as he stood there, gazing at her with an expression of fondness he shouldn't be wearing.

"What?" She sat up and blinked, not wanting to rub her eyes in front of him or stretch, though she was certain that would help her to get her faculties back into place.

"Aye, ye've been missing for a couple of hours now. And I'm afraid your sister and mother have eaten all the biscuits."

Biscuits? What biscuits?

Poppy bolted up to her feet, shaking the cobwebs of sleep from her brain, and gathered her blanket and book. "What do you mean?"

"They went looking for ye during tea, and when they couldn't find ye, sent out a party to search. All your servants, Colonel Austen, me. I'm glad I found ye."

"I wasn't lost. Just napping."

"Well, I think that's what they make beds for," he teased, but it only made her bristle.

Because they made beds for other things. Things she thought they might do together until Dougal had dashed those thoughts, and all she could think of now was him and Lucia doing those same things.

"Though I canna blame ye," Dougal said. "The weather is enchanting, and I have had more than a few naps against a tree."

Oh, now he would ruin her afternoon napping sessions too? She'd never be able to lean against a tree without thinking of him again. Poppy rushed back toward the cottage, irritated that it had been Dougal who found her, woke her, and now kept stride with her.

"Don't you have somewhere to be?" she asked, hoping her tone would be more than a hint he should shoo like a fly.

"I'm right where I want to be."

Oh! The nerve! How dare he say such a thing. With her usual wit and a bit of snark, she said, "Rushing over the grass?"

"With Miss Featherstone, ye forgot to add that." He seemed unbothered by her obvious irritation with him, which only made her more irritated.

"Is that a choice that most people would make? Like biscuits with milk or toast and jam? A walk with a woman they've..." She couldn't finish the sentence; even uttering it made her feel shame.

Dougal stopped walking. She spied him reaching for her elbow and hurried forward. Felt him staring at her retreating back as he said, "Doesna matter, Poppy. Ye're no' most people, and neither am I. However, it is the choice that I'm making."

That made her feet stop working, her legs halting in place. He was making the choice to be there with her. Not with Lucia. It was too much. All of it. Too much and not enough. And so much she couldn't even understand or put words to. As if she'd lost the ability to form thoughts and reason.

Poppy did the best thing she knew how to—she ran. Hurrying away from him, hurrying from the feelings he brought out. But the clouds of confusion followed, and the ache in her chest seized her.

Her heart begged her to turn around, to acknowledge what he'd said, and then demand to know everything.

In the distance, she could hear people calling her name.

Understood then that their worry for her outweighed her sentiments where Dougal was concerned. She could give him a piece of her mind and demand answers later, after she let her mother know that she'd not been eaten by wolves, though to be honest, when she was beside Dougal, that was a little how she felt.

Devoured, torn.

Back at the cottage, her mother broke out into singsong pleasure upon seeing her arrival, and Anise let out a long breath.

And behind her, she could hear the very distinct sounds of Dougal approaching.

16

D ougal bristled with frustration.

The entire point of his coming today had been to speak the truth, and he'd done a slapdash job at that. When he'd finally blurted out that being with Poppy was the only place he wanted to be, he could see he'd struck a chord in her, but then she'd run off. He couldn't decide whether she'd run off in disgust or she'd run off to put distance between them for her to think.

Part of his mind, the more reasonable part, instructed him to give her time to mull over what he'd said. After all, prior to his arrival, she'd likely cursed him to the darkest depths of the Hell. The other part told him to bolt after her and demand she listen because he was afraid of losing her. Afraid that he'd already wasted too much time not telling her how he felt.

Dougal reached the charming cottage, which was clear the women had been working hard to bring back to life, to hear the sounds through an open window of Lady Cullen cooing over Poppy and Anise fussing too.

Colonel Austen was standing in the center of the yard,

looking as confused as a puppy in the rain. His friend eyed him as though he had something to say but couldn't remember how to make his mouth work.

"Out with it," Dougal demanded under his breath when he reached his side.

"Did ye tell her?"

Dougal grimaced. "I tried, but I hardly had the chance." He gestured toward the women, seen now through the drawing room window. They were hugging as though Poppy had disappeared well and truly for days and not merely hours. "Couldna get in the way of that reunion." Mentally, he nailed his feet in place, else he would march inside.

Austen nodded, looking slightly crestfallen. "Anise talked of nothing but Sir John the entire time we searched for Poppy."

Dougal grimaced. That must have been painful for his friend, who had most certainly found himself in love with the youngest Featherstone. "Saints, but she doesna realize what an arse he is."

"She will." Dougal's tone alluded to a confidence he didn't feel. What he was coming to understand in the past few weeks was that he didn't understand women at all.

"How so?"

Dougal cleared his throat, trying to reason it out himself. Then, he recalled a detail that Austen might not yet know. "The lad's gone off to France."

"He has?" Austen turned to face him, little lines of hope creasing the corners of his eyes.

Dougal was glad he could bring his friend some solace here. "Facing criminal charges. It'll be in the papers tonight, I'm certain."

Dougal wondered, did the ladies even get a newspaper?

Not that he'd sat with them for days on end, but the times

he had, he didn't recall them reading anything other than books.

"We'll need to make certain they see it." Colonel Austen was standing straighter, then suddenly slumped. "It will break her heart."

Dougal understood his friend's dilemma. For his own bad news had broken Poppy's heart. "But ye'll be there to pick up the pieces."

"I will. And ye?"

"Unfortunately, Lucia has no' committed any crimes that I know of, besides wearing a brooch that allegedly contains a lock of my hair I'm no' certain how she obtained." Dougal still found that piece of information disturbing.

"Shame and also odd." Austen grinned.

"Aye, it would make this easier if Lucia had committed a crime, but alas, I do believe she is at the mercy of Campbell and has been compromised, which is no' her fault. I've told Poppy I'm no' betrothed, and I've told her I want to be here with her, but she's tossed me off at both declarations. I admit they were no' perhaps the most eloquent."

"Ye need to speak with her again."

"Aye." Dougal's gaze strayed back toward the window where the three women had sat down, none the wiser that the two men stood outside their window talking about them.

"Alone," Austen said.

"Aye." Dougal drew out the word. How the hell was he supposed to do that?

As if reading his thoughts, Austen said, "I will provide a distraction."

"Will ye now?" Dougal grinned at his friend.

"Aye. And perhaps we'll also discover a newspaper while we're about."

"Two birds, one stone?"

"Something like that." Colonel Austen left his side and let himself into the cottage, and Dougal watched him approach the ladies through the window.

Not to be left behind, Dougal hurried inside the cottage as well in time to hear Austen say, "Miss Anise, I have yet to try the creamery I saw in the village last night as we passed through. Have ye tried it yet?"

Anise blinked at him, her face a mystery as to what she was thinking. "A creamery?"

"Would ye care to join me? Ye and Lady Cullen?" Austen bowed slightly to the baroness.

"Aye, that would be delightful," Lady Cullen said, glancing at Poppy, who had not been included in the invitation.

Poppy glanced toward Dougal, her eyes slightly widening as her clever mind put together what was happening.

"Lord Reay asked to take a walk by the seaside, and I think I shall oblige him ." Poppy surprised him by voicing the mistruth. Though she wasn't wrong, he did want to walk alone with her by the seaside; he just hadn't been able to ask her yet.

"Oh," Lady Cullen said, glancing toward Dougal, her eyes narrowing a bit.

"I promise to take good care of your daughter," he said. "No seaside calamities on my watch."

Lady Cullen nodded. "I believe you, sir. Shall I call for our curricle, then?"

As the trio waited for the horses to be rigged up to the curricle, Dougal offered his arm to Poppy. She didn't take it, but she did walk beside him, and that was a huge win in his book.

They meandered away from the cottage, heading toward the sea-salt air of the cliffs. He contemplated at least thirty different ways to open the conversation and found each lacking.

"And what if I had said I wanted iced cream?" she asked, breaking the silence.

"I'd have gone with ye there."

"But you clearly wanted to get me alone." Was that a hint of teasing he heard in her tone?

"Dinna make it sound so nefarious, Miss Featherstone. I just wanted to talk."

"I'm listening."

Dougal had one chance to get this right, and he needed to tread carefully because if he failed now, there was no telling if she'd give him another shot. "I didna lie when I said I was no' engaged. And I didna lie when I said the only place I wanted to be was by your side."

Even though they did not touch, the air around her seemed to stiffen, and he could sense her shoring up her fortifications against anything he might say.

"Allow me to share a story of a foolish youth?" he asked.

"Sounds entertaining." She shrugged, and it was hard for him to get a full read on her tone.

Dougal grinned hopefully. "Entertaining if ye are no' me. Nearly ten years ago, I was deep in my cups with a bunch of lads from school. We were carousing harder than we should have. And a few ladies had sneaked out to partake with us. I think with the added feminine presence, we might have been competing a bit for attention."

Poppy gasped, and she glanced over at him, truly shocked. "Ladies? Alone? Drinking spirits?"

"Aye. It happens, though 'tis rare. Nothing untoward in the physical sense, but they did drink and dance, and mostly it was fun. But that night, I decided I was in love with one of them. And I told her that if I'd no' married by my twenty-ninth birthday, we should we. She agreed. I admit to being a total idiot, though at least I was an idiot who didna want to be tied down immediately." There, he'd said it, given her the entire sordid, stupid truth.

Poppy remained silent for a few moments, mulling over what he'd said, no doubt. "And how old are you now?"

"Twenty-eight."

"And your birthday?"

"Less than two weeks."

"Ah." Poppy drawled out the sound. "So, she has come calling."

Dougal let out a sigh, glad that Poppy seemed to understand exactly what he was trying to relay. "She has. I found out she was invited by my sister. I suspect for other reasons as well."

"Mary invited her?" Now Poppy looked annoyed.

"Aye, though I didn't know that before. I thought Lucia had only sent a letter to my aunt."

Poppy was silent, and when he glanced her way, he could see she was staring at the ground as they walked, her steps getting slower, brow furrowed.

"Why?" She glanced up at him, her nose wrinkled. "Why would Mary do that?"

Dougal let out a long sigh. "I have no idea. It's hard to guess the reason behind most of my sister's actions. Sometimes she's a gem, a real sweetheart, but those moments are so..."

"Rare?"

"Aye."

"Is she friends with Lucia? Maybe she wants to see you happy and believes the union would do that."

Her willingness to see the good in people was one of the reasons Dougal adored her. "That is verra charitable of ye to say."

"Which part? That Lucia would make you happy or that Mary wants it for you?"

"All of it." Dougal let out a long sigh. "Whatever Mary's reasons are, Lucia is no' going to make me happy." He stopped walking then, turning and taking her hands in his. She didn't pull away. "No' when I'm in love with someone else."

Poppy's eyes widened. "Who?"

"Oh, dear heavens, woman, *ye*."

Her throat bobbed as she swallowed, her eyes glistening as she blinked. "You love me?"

"I have from the moment I met ye. And I'm ashamed it has taken me so long to say it. I was scared. Afraid I wasna going to live up to what ye deserve in a man, a husband. And I ran. I ran from ye, I ran from a future with ye, and I ran from my own happiness."

"You love me," she said again, but this time it wasn't a question. "All this time."

"Aye."

She laughed softly. "You really are an idiot."

Dougal was stunned by her words until he saw the spark of mischief in her eyes. "Perhaps I am, but this idiot has fallen completely head over heels for ye."

Her laughter died down, and she gave him a serious look. "I'd be an idiot to marry an idiot."

"Ye're the smartest woman I've ever met."

"Alas, it's true. I do have a brain, though it's currently turned to mush."

Dougal dropped to his knees, her hands still clasped in

his. "Poppy Featherstone, will ye do me the honor of becoming my wife?"

She pursed her lips, eyeing him. "By what birthday? Thirty-nine?

"Today, right now."

She laughed. "Oh no, you'll not get out of this so easily."

"No?"

"I have lived the last year thinking I did something wrong. Then you came waltzing back into my life, and I thought maybe you'd changed your mind, only to find out you were engaged to another." For all she was saying, she didn't let go of his hands, and Dougal took that as a good sign as he listened. "It's going to take a lot more than you getting on your knees for me to say yes. Although, I will say, I do rather like seeing you in this position."

Dougal bit back a laugh, knowing this moment, though she'd added a tease, called for sincerity. "Anything. What do I have to do to prove to ye that I'm here, for ye, always?"

Poppy straightened her shoulders as she made her request. "I want to be wooed."

"I will woo ye until the end of our days together."

"Courted."

"I will never stop courting ye because even when we say I do, I want to win your affections every day that I'm lucky to call ye mine."

"My, you're good at this." Her lips curled. "I want to feel..."

"Important?"

"Desired."

Dougal stood then, tugging her toward him, holding her hands to his chest. "Poppy, I desire ye more than any woman I've ever encountered. Ye are exquisite. Your lips have the flavor of strawberry iced cream. So delicious that I could never desire to stray. I've no' kissed another since the moment I kissed ye in the gardens last year."

Her cheeks flushed pink.

"I desire your mind, your laugh, your gaze. I desire your kiss, the feel of your body against mine."

She gasped slightly.

"Dinna doubt my desire for ye, I beg ye. And there is nothing more important in my life than ye. 'Tis why I dropped everything in Edinburgh to chase after ye. I ran from ye once, and I'll never do it again. From this day forward, wherever ye are is where I want to be."

"I wanted to believe you when you said that earlier."

"Do ye believe me now?" He cupped the side of her face, stroking her soft skin with the pad of his thumb. "I want ye to trust me. I'll do whatever it takes to prove that I'm true."

Poppy stared into his eyes. "I want to."

"'Tis all right if ye're still a little skeptical. I will make it my mission to change your mind and solidify my trustworthiness."

She nodded. "I'm..." She let out a breath. "I admit to being overwhelmed. So much has changed in so little time, and it's hard to grasp all of it."

"I can understand that."

"My father's death. Leaving my childhood home. Being unwelcome in Edward's home. You being back in my life." She shook her head and swiped at a tear that slipped from the corner of her eye. "Sometimes it just feels as if the things I want are only fleeting."

Dougal nodded. "I canna bring your father back. Nor your childhood home. I canna change Mary or Edward, though I would happily try. What I can offer and give freely and lavishly is my love, a new home to make your own, and anything else ye might ask of me."

"Thank you, Dougal." She did smile then. "You're making good on your promise to woo me."

"This is only the start."

With her face turned up to his, Dougal wanted nothing more than to kiss her. To feel the lips he'd dreamed about for a year against his own. To taste the sugary sweetness of her mouth, the soft sighs of her breath on his face. He cupped her cheek, swiping his thumb over the soft arch, the tiny smatter of freckles.

"I want—"

But before he could finish his statement of desiring to kiss her, Poppy leaned on her tiptoes, tossed her arms around his shoulders and pressed her mouth to his.

☙❧

Poppy thought, too late, of course, that she probably shouldn't be kissing Dougal. She'd asked him to court her, woo her, prove to her that he was true, and now here, she'd gone and pressed her lips to his.

The kiss was sweet at first, a softness giving way to something deeper, something hungrier. The year that spanned their last kiss and this moment melted away as they sighed into each other, the familiar feel of his mouth sliding over hers, his breath on her face.

And the all too familiar coil of heat in her belly, the curl of her toes in her slippers and her fingers against his jacket. How a simple kiss could ignite flames inside her was puzzling, but a puzzle she didn't feel she needed to solve, only one to keep in pieces where it would remain mysterious and cloying.

Dougal's arms came around her waist, the weight of his

muscled limbs sinking into her frame like the comfort and spark of a long-lost lover. She imagined herself a heroine from a book, her lover gone so long at sea he had been feared dead, only to walk out of the ocean in one piece and fall to his knees before her.

This was going to be their fairy tale ending. This kiss on a salt-spray cliff, with the sounds of birds hovering in the clouds and the ocean crashing against the rocky crag. She would be quite happy to remain here forever. To make this very spot their world and his lips her home.

But just as all fairy tales come to an end, so, too, did her happy imaginings, as she picked up on something that Dougal had said earlier.

He had to marry by his twenty-ninth birthday, which was a fortnight away.

Doubt started to creep in. Was he only wooing her, kissing her, to get her to say yes because she was a better option than Lucia Steventon?

"What's wrong?" Dougal's hands pressed to her cheeks, his hooded gaze on hers, as he pulled away from their kiss to meet her eyes.

Poppy bit her lower lip, holding in her mind's fearful road.

"Poppy, please. Tell me."

"You need to marry by your twenty-ninth birthday. Am I just a convenient choice?"

Dougal groaned. His hands slipped from her face but didn't leave her as they settled on her shoulders.

His eyes bore into hers, staid. "Nay. I wouldna, or willna, or anything other w-word, marry Lucia, whether ye were to agree to be my wife or no'."

"And I have yet to agree," she reminded him, just in case.

"I know." He said it softly, a small smile on his lips. "And even if it takes to my thirty-ninth or forty-ninth to get ye to agree, I willna stop trying."

"Then I may make you wait."

"If that's what it takes."

She nodded. "What are the consequences?"

"There are none. My inheritance is not linked to my birthday, only that I do eventually provide an heir. Lucia's insistence that we are betrothed is based on a drunken suggestion. Claiming witnesses, but they were all as inebriated as I was, and she'd also have to admit she had been behaving improperly, which would be an embarrassment to her father. Furthermore, I have reason to suspect her prior engagement to a rival of mine at Oxford may have compromised her, and he denied her, so she's grasping at straws."

Poppy's hand rested over his heart. "You're much more than a stalk of straw."

"I agree." He smiled. "I'm at least a thistle or an oak."

"Definitely a pine." Poppy's smile faltered. "All jesting aside, Dougal. Does Lucia know that you will not marry her?"

"I've told her and her father as much. And my solicitor has also now gotten involved." He let out a long sigh. "In fact, I'm awaiting news from my solicitor as to the results of said confrontation. While Lucia is grasping and likely a fallen woman, I in no way want to further besmirch her reputation. I merely had my solicitor inform her father that there would be no offer of marriage. And then, in a note as gently and delicately as I could, reminded her of how our connection, and lack thereof, came to be. If she were so inclined to have a solicitor prepare legal documents, she should go after Campbell himself, not me."

"Her prior fiancé?"

"Aye."

"And the father of her child?"

"I canna confirm if she's with child or if Campbell is the father, but it is what I suspect."

"What a shame she would try to dupe you." Poppy frowned.

"Aye. But I'd no' be the first scapegoat. Besides," he tucked a lock of her hair behind her ear, "none of that matters, no' when I have ye."

17

P oppy could have remained where she stood for the rest of the day, the week, the month, contemplating everything that had happened, changed, in the last hour.

Dougal loved her.

Dougal was vulnerable. Opening up to how he'd run away from her, from London, in fear. She was still mad about it. A year of misery when they could have had a simple conversation, but the fact that he was opening up to her about it now meant the world to her. And she was open to forgiving him.

Dougal had pledged his life to her.

To *her*. Poppy Featherstone. *She* was the woman Dougal Mackay placed upon a pedestal.

As they turned to head back toward the cottage, she had to pinch herself. Was this really happening? The pinch stung, and so she wasn't asleep. Good sign. That meant the kiss, his declaration, his promises were all real.

Dougal tucked her arm around his elbow as they walked, the flex of his muscles beneath her hand enticing her to gently squeeze. He flexed again and grinned down at her.

As the cottage came into view, Dougal paused his steps, and she, too, came to a stop.

"What is it?" Fragile still, she saw her current bliss coming to an end.

"There is something ye should know afore we get inside and greet your sister and mother." Dougal's expression had turned grave, and Poppy felt suddenly ill.

Pressing a hand to her belly, she said, "Tell me."

"'Tis about Sir John, and Anise is bound to be heartbroken." Dougal glanced at her, his face full of regret for whatever he was about to relay.

"Was she so obvious in her...affection for him?" Poppy's cheeks colored.

"I may have heard about it or noticed it." Dougal smiled, though it was filled with a sadness Poppy wished she didn't have to see.

"She fancies herself in love with him, but I don't trust him," she admitted.

"And with good reason." Dougal rubbed a hand over his face. "There will be things written in the newspaper about him. He's been accused of...damaging a few ladies' reputations. Charged with criminal conversation."

Poppy's eyes widened. Oh, dear heavens, it was worse than she thought. And Anise—had she been one of those ladies? She didn't think they'd been alone too often, but Poppy had been preoccupied with her grief.

"He's..." Dougal pressed his lips together to stop himself from saying another word.

"He's what?" she urged.

Dougal looked so conflicted, and she imagined he was searching for the right words. "He has a disease."

Poppy gasped. Poor Sir John! Flashes of their friend home

in bed, wasting away, came into her mind. "Oh no, what kind of disease?"

Poppy had to blink as she watched Dougal, one of the manliest men she'd ever come across, blush.

"The kind that passes between a man and a woman." Judging by the tight guttural sounds, he practically choked on the words as he said them.

"Oh, my goodness." Poppy's cheeks might as well have burst into flames for all the heat she felt in them, and now she understood why Dougal was blushing. "Like Henry VIII?"

"Exactly." He looked relieved that he wouldn't have to explain further.

"And well, there has been one death associated with his... affections."

"What? A death? She wasn't treated?"

"She hid her illness, and so no, was no' treated. And came down with a fever from one of the sores becoming infected. And then, well, she passed."

Poppy's heart seized in her chest. The poor creature. "My... That is so awful."

"Verra." Dougal's face was grim, his lips set in a straight line. He looked off into the distance for a moment and she wanted to know what he was thinking but was too nervous to ask.

But she did need to clarify one thing. "And you're sure it was Sir John?"

Dougal nodded grimly. "Aye. He fled. I suspect he'll no' be back to Scotland, or England for that matter."

Poppy's hand came to her chest, and she swallowed hard, her attention drawn to the curricle coming around a bend in the road as they returned from the village iced cream excursion. The vehicle, thank heavens, held her sister, who she hoped was safe from the affliction Sir John had so callously passed on to others.

"She is going to be heartbroken," Poppy whispered.

"Aye."

"Does Colonel Austen know?" she asked.

"Aye, and he loves her."

Poppy nodded. "I thought as much. She had esteem for Colonel Austen, too, before Sir John came about."

"Then perhaps he will be able to woo her back to him."

"Perhaps."

They hurried back to the cottage in silence so they might meet the trio as they dismounted from the curricle. They both worried about what was going to happen when the three arrived. Had Anise already found out about Sir John? Should Poppy tell her sister?

What kind of a question was that? She should definitely tell Anise. The man might have compromised her, too, if he'd not run off after last night's dance. That also explained why he'd not come to call today. And why had Anise had been so eager to visit the village with the colonel? She likely hoped to spy Sir John, which would have been fruitless. And if she'd seen a newspaper...

They'd just arrived at the front yard of the cottage when the colonel rushed out, and screeching from inside filled the air.

"What's happened?" Poppy asked, though she thought she might know the answer.

Colonel Austen blanched and looked full of regret, though Sir John's situation was not his fault. "Your sister is distraught. Rather sad news, I'm afraid, about—"

"Sir John," Poppy finished.

"Aye." He cast his eyes toward Dougal, who nodded.

"How did she find out?" Poppy asked.

"I regret that it was wagging tongues. I'd hoped to inform her more gently."

"Not a newspaper?"

Austen shook his head. "Just town gossip at the creamery," he said with a grimace and turned back toward the house at the sound of a crash.

Both men started to run for the door, but Poppy rushed in front of them, stopping them with a hand on both their chests. It'd been years since her sister threw a tantrum that resulted in breaking items, but it appeared Anise's disagreeable habit was returning, and she was not about to let it be witnessed.

"Just a little bout of...upset," Poppy said with a forced smile. "Best you leave this to my mother and me. And perhaps come by tomorrow for tea?"

Both men looked stricken, neither wanting to leave for different reasons, she was sure, but witnessing her sister have an epic tantrum was not exactly the memory she wanted them to have. Already, the screeching and crashing were embarrassing enough.

Dougal nodded first, followed by the colonel.

"Tomorrow," Dougal said. "We'll come for tea."

"Aye," Colonel Austen agreed, his eyes on a window to the left, where Poppy hoped the shades were drawn.

"Have a good evening," Poppy said, giving them the tiniest nudge with her fingers to go.

They doffed their hats, retreating to their horses, and she didn't wait to see them go before she whirled around and entered the house. Anise was shouting and sobbing in the drawing room, and their mother's words were drowned out by the noise.

Poppy opened the drawing room door to see that several

precious books had been thrown—the crashes they'd heard—along with a vase of flowers.

Anise rounded on her sister. "Oh, Poppy, the worst has come to pass."

Poppy did not believe this was the worst. She could name several other more terrible things that had happened to them in the past few months, but she didn't say that. Instead, she picked up the mess as she asked, "What's happened?"

"Sir John has gone! Fled the country, and I'll likely never see him again!" she wailed.

That was the worst? She didn't care that he carried a disease that killed a woman? That he'd been spreading himself over all of Britain and leaving a wake of illness behind him?

But perhaps Anise didn't know that part. It was a rather delicate subject.

Before Poppy could try and explain what had happened with Sir John, Anise fled the room, leaving her with their mother to stare after the space she'd occupied.

"Mama," Poppy said, "there's more to the story."

Mama sighed. "I know. When Anise and the colonel were getting into the curricle, I pretended to have left my gloves in the creamery. I went back inside and asked the gossiping crowd what had happened."

"Then you know he wasn't honorable."

"I do." Her mother's nod was resigned. "But how did you?"

"Dougal told me while we were on our walk."

"Ah. A shame, but I'm glad we found out before it was too late. Could you imagine?" Mama's fan popped out of her sleeve and opened to fan off her reddening cheeks. It wasn't a question so much as an invitation to view the horrors of what could have come to pass.

"We must count our blessings that we found out when we did." Poppy sent up a silent prayer of thanks.

"Indeed." Mama sank onto one of the chairs. "I'm so disappointed, though. I had high hopes that she would make a match."

"She might yet. The colonel seems to fancy her."

"Aye, but I'm not so certain your sister fancies the colonel."

Poppy nodded. "Time will tell."

"Mmm."

❄

THE FOLLOWING MORNING, ANISE DID NOT COME TO breakfast, and Poppy and her mother seemed resigned to allowing her a day to feel better.

At tea, when Dougal and the colonel arrived, she still refused to come down. Not even the biscuits Dougal brought could entice her, nor the stack of new books the colonel brought for them to read.

After an hour, when it was apparent she would not be making an appearance, the colonel begged his leave, and Dougal offered to go on a walk with Poppy, who claimed she needed fresh air.

"How is your sister?" he asked when they were out of earshot of the cottage.

"Mourning."

"Sir John has that effect on people."

"So it seems. They hardly knew one another, so I'm not sure she so much mourns him as a person as she mourns the life she dreamed she'd have. Moving to Skerray has been an adjustment for us all, but it's been hardest on Anise."

"How are ye faring?" Dougal searched her face when she gazed at him, and his concern warmed her heart.

Poppy flashed him a smile. "Better than my sister. But I prefer the outdoors like this. I find peace in it, and she'd rather find peace at a party or lady's luncheon."

"This new life must be hard for her then."

"I believe it is."

"What is the life ye dream of having?" Dougal asked.

Poppy opened her mouth, thinking she had an answer, but then closed it again, her gaze on the rippling water over the cliff's edge they walked along. "I thought I used to know what I wanted. Now I'm not so sure."

"What did ye used to want?"

They came to an outcropping of rocks, and Poppy perched on one, Dougal beside her.

"I used to want a life very much like what we had. A townhouse in Edinburgh, another in London. Country houses in the north of England and the Highlands of Scotland. Traveling from one place to another with an endless calendar of fun."

"Sounds amusing," he smiled.

"It is, to a degree. But then we came here, and life is slower, simpler, calmer. And," she gestured toward the sea, "there is this incredible view I never knew I wanted to sit and stare at for hours."

"And your desire for what ye want in life has changed."

She nodded. "I still don't know what that looks like, but perhaps something in between."

"Castle Varrich sits on a coastal cliff." She could tell he was trying to entice her by his expression.

"Does it?" She cocked her head to the side, a small smile on her lips.

"Aye, over the Kyle of Tongue. With a view of the mountains, Ben Loyal and Ben Hope."

Poppy sighed, imagining what it would be like to wake up to a view like that every morning. "I like the sounds of those mountains. Loyal and Hope, the things that bring us peace."

"Aye." Dougal smiled. "'Tis peaceful there, breathtaking. I think ye'd like it."

"Then perhaps we ought to visit?"

"I would be happy to bring ye for a visit."

"And maybe Anise too?" she asked. "To get her out of her melancholy. A castle might do the trick."

Dougal nodded. "What it doesna do, the mountains might."

They walked back to the house, but before they arrived, he tugged her behind a tree, pressing his spine against it and tugging her close enough to smell the delicious pine scent of him.

Dougal glanced down at her mouth, and she suddenly knew what he wanted. The same thing she did. A kiss.

She closed her eyes as he leaned toward her, soaking up the feel of his lips brushing over hers. Every part of her came alive with the touch of lips on lips. Tingles, shivers and a wicked heat pooled in her belly. Poppy lifted her arms around his shoulders to bring herself closer. Dougal's hands cupped her face, and he deepened the kiss with a swipe of his tongue over her lower lip and then began to duel with hers.

As swiftly as his kiss had begun, it ended. She stared up at him, a little dazed.

"Something to remember me by." And he tucked a small yellow flower behind her ear; she hadn't even realized he'd picked one.

"I could never forget you, Dougal. I'll see you tomorrow."

"A picnic by the water."

"Sounds like heaven." And she imagined there might be more kisses like this one.

The following day, after breakfast, a carriage arrived from Castle Varrich for the ladies to make their way. Mama begged her pardon, remaining behind and sending Poppy and Anise off without her.

The journey was less than an hour, and the sun shone on the water of the Kyle of Tongue and spread golden fingers through the forests covering the mountains.

"'Tis beautiful," Poppy murmured.

Anise had yet to recover, eyes puffy, mouth frowning, but even she couldn't help peering out the window of the carriage at the breathtaking landscape.

"I never thought when coming out to the Highlands for our house arrest that we'd be spending the day at a castle." Her bemused mention of the castle softened the slight sarcasm of her statement about their imprisonment.

"I'm grateful for those we know."

"I'm just glad he didn't turn out to be a world-class jack-ass," Anise said, raising a brow at her sister. "Not like the one I fell for."

"Sir John was charming and handsome. It's not your fault he duped you."

"Oh, Poppy, you can say that all you want, but I should have seen past the charm."

"There's no way you could have. He wouldn't let you."

Anise rolled her eyes. "I'll never fall for another man like that again. Maybe no man at all. I'll just let myself age up into a dried prune of a spinster and live out my life taking care of Mama until we both perish."

Poppy refrained from rolling her eyes. Anise was doing a fabulous "Woe is me" job, and she hoped she stopped before the carriage did. Today was supposed to be fun, not sour.

Dougal was waiting for them outside the castle, a large dog sitting stoically beside him. Poppy couldn't help but smile as the carriage door opened and she hopped down.

"Who is this?" she asked, offering her hand to the dog for a sniff.

"This is Sentry."

"Oh, a perfect name for a brave guard dog."

Sentry gave her a lick on her hand, and she found herself crouching before him to scratch behind his ears and coo.

"All that cooing, and he'll be no good at guarding, only wanting the love of a woman."

"Did your superior officers say that to you?" she teased as she glanced up at Dougal.

Dougal laughed hard, his head falling back with the force of it, and then they both turned to see Anise, who had finally decided to climb out of the carriage.

She looked up at the large castle walls and the windows that glistened in the sun. "You have a lovely castle, Lord Reay."

"Thank ye, Miss Anise. One I'm happy to share with friends."

She smiled tightly at Dougal. "I appreciate your generosity."

The door opened then with the colonel rushing from inside the castle. "I do apologize for no' being here to greet ye," he said, "I had a letter to finish that was most urgent." As if to punctuate that, a footman rode off on horseback from around the side of the castle.

"Colonel Austen," Anise said. The light that had been dull and faded in her eyes was somewhat lightening. "This is a pleasant surprise. I didn't realize you'd be here."

"Ah, aye," he said. "I've been staying with Dougal."

This was knowledge that had been shared upon their first

visit, but Anise, too enamored with thoughts of Sir John, must not have listened.

"That's lovely to have such good friends." Anise's smile was sad, and she likely thought of the friends she'd had to leave behind.

Perhaps Poppy should write to them and invite them for a stay. Their house was rather small, but if she and Anise bunked up, they could have at least two in the other room.

The idea had merit, and she'd need to think more about it. Whatever to get her sister out of her melancholy.

"'Tis such a beautiful day. Shall we take Sentry for a walk by the Kyle?" Dougal said. "He does love to chase sticks in the water."

"I would love to see your property and to throw a stick."

Sentry took off running around the side of the castle on a path that led to Kyle, and the four of them followed, Dougal and Poppy in the front and Anise at a much slower pace behind.

Though her sister was rather melancholy, there had at least been a spark upon seeing the colonel. A familiar and trusted face. Perhaps that was just what her sister needed to get her moving toward the light again.

18

She was here.

Dougal's fingers tingled with the need to lace them through Poppy's. To tug her toward him and kiss her. To tell her again how much he loved her. Somehow, miraculously really, he was able to contain himself as they meandered down the well-worn path from the castle to the water's edge.

The Kyle of Tongue was smooth today, high tide, and he hoped that the calmness of the water somehow seeped into his bones.

The very thing he'd known he'd wanted for the better part of a year—a life with Poppy—was on the verge of becoming a reality.

Poppy bent beside him and picked up a stick that had already been properly chewed on one end by Sentry. She didn't avoid the obviously slobbered wood as she tossed it a dozen or more yards away, which Dougal found endearing. She must like dogs, and that was a huge bonus for him.

Sentry barked and took off running, intent on maiming the stick once more.

"He's a rather rambunctious fellow, isn't he?" she said with a laugh, watching as Sentry bounded toward the stick, then somersaulted over the downed limb, grabbing and shaking the life from it before he ran back toward them.

"That he is."

"Come here, boy," Poppy called, clapping her hands.

"Do ye like dogs?" he asked.

"Oh, yes." Poppy's eyes lit up. "We never had one, but I always liked playing with my friends' and neighbors' dogs."

"Why's it that ye never had one?"

"Oh, they made Papa sneeze something fierce. Anytime he went around them, it would start a fit. He couldn't even enjoy a good hunt, and his sneezing scared off all the prey, so he was hardly invited out."

"That is unfortunate. But ye and your sister didna inherit the sneezing affliction?"

"Oh, I sneeze plenty," she laughed, followed by a tiny sneeze. "But not as bad as my Papa, and I'm also not going to ruin a hunt. And more to the point, I don't care. I'd sneeze all day just to play or cuddle."

Anise laughed at something the colonel said, drawing both of their attention toward the couple.

"I do hope your sister is...feeling better," Dougal said.

"She is," Poppy assured him. "And I think the attention the colonel pays her is a balm to her heart. Rather than think about what Sir John had done, she was more concerned with herself, that maybe it had been her that pushed Sir John away. Mama didn't want to tell her the part about his disease just yet. Thought it might be too delicate. I think she'll realize the truth eventually, but seeing that another man is interested in her is good. I only worry that she might be too fickle for your colonel friend."

"Och, Austen can take care of himself. I'm just glad she's

out and about rather than hiding." Dougal winced as soon as he said it, recalling that hiding had been exactly what Poppy had done a few days before.

"Everyone needs time to adjust." She shrugged.

"I didna mean to offend."

She smiled at him. "You did nothing of the sort. I thought you were referring to your yearlong escape."

Dougal laughed. "Touché. Your hiding for one day this week hardly compares."

"Exactly." Her eyes danced with merriment. "I am glad we've both decided to face each other and whatever there might be between us."

"I am too."

This time, Dougal picked up the stick. He tossed it over the colonel's head, sending Sentry barreling down the water's edge and splashing Austen and Anise. Anise squealed, her arms flailing, and the colonel swooped in, lifting her in his arms and carrying her away from the splashing dog.

"Did you do that on purpose?" Poppy asked.

"Maybe." Dougal smirked.

"Rogue," she teased.

Dougal grinned. "They might have needed a push. Look at them now."

Anise had her arms around the colonel's shoulders and was gazing at him as he cradled her to his frame in a way that was both inspiring and endearing.

"What a matchmaker you are," Poppy said with a light laugh. "Though to be fair, my friend Lady Ava, daughter of Earl of Heatherfield, is by far the best matchmaker in this country."

"Oh, is that so?"

"Only one or two of her attempts have ended in disaster.

The rest give stellar reviews." The tinkle of Poppy's laugh was infectious.

Dougal chuckled. "I actually think I've heard of her. But she's no' yet wed herself."

"No. Been out a few seasons. She's a year older than me and has yet to find a man she is willing to devote the rest of her life to. Though to be honest, I think she's focusing on finding love matches for other people so she can avoid her own happiness."

"I know something of avoiding happiness."

Poppy stared up at him, her eyes searching his. "But no longer?"

"I refuse to avoid it. I am facing happiness head-on. Right now. Forever."

Her lips curled up, a teasing glint in her eyes. "Shall I change my name to happiness then?"

Dougal wanted to reach out and stroke her cheek, but feared doing so in front of the others, then thought, what the hell? He did it anyway, mesmerized by the smoothness of her skin, cooled only slightly by the Highland air. "Nay, Poppy suits ye perfectly."

She leaned into his caress. "Since when did you become so dashing?"

"The moment I met ye."

"Flatterer." Her eyes danced.

"When it comes to ye, sweet Poppy, I will flatter until I have no breath left in my body." He wrapped around his finger a lock of hair not pulled back into her low knot.

"Your wooing is quite good."

"The more I practice, the better it will be. Like kissing," he drawled.

"Is that so?" Her gaze slid to his mouth, and desire pooled in his gut. "Should we...practice?"

Dougal nearly choked at her bold suggestion, for he very much wanted to tug her into his embrace. "I think it is only fair—"

But just then, Sentry crashed into the back of Dougal's legs, causing his knees to buckle, and though he caught himself before he stumbled, it wasn't before he reached forward and accidentally pressed his hands to Poppy's breasts to catch his balance.

Her mouth popped open, and so did his as they both stared down at her chest with his hands splayed over her bosom. They were ample and soft, and he wanted nothing more than to massage them. To bend down and kiss them. This reminded him of those moments in the garden a year ago where he'd brushed his palms over her taut nipples.

"Dougal," she said.

"Ah, sorry about that." He yanked his hands away, a pain in itself when he was perfectly happy there. Impossible, but his face flamed with heat. "Did they see?" He didn't want to look behind him at the colonel and Anise.

"Thankfully, no."

"Please do accept my apologies for, uh...touching ye inappropriately."

"Well, it was an accident, and also...it is only inappropriate if I didn't want you to touch me."

Dougal groaned. "Poppy..."

"This walk has too much open space. You should have suggested the woods." Her pout was put on.

He chuckled. "I would relish the chance to ravish ye against a tree."

Poppy's eyes flashed with a yearning he felt deep in his bones. "I want to be ravished."

"I can make that happen," he said in a gravelly and tight voice.

Dougal let out a low whistle. Not only did Sentry come to his side, but a footman appeared from where he'd been posted by the castle, and Sentry obeyed Dougal's command to follow the footman for the rest of his walk.

Then he turned to the colonel and Anise. "Shall I show ye my garden maze? It was built by my great-grandmother. We can get lost in there for hours." He turned to Poppy and winked, watching in fascination as her cheeks pinkened.

He leaned low. "I think we might have a tree in the garden...or at the verra least, a bench."

"Oh," she murmured, half-sigh, half-gasp.

BEING IN A PLAYFUL MOOD, ANISE RAN AHEAD TO THE maze, and the colonel shot Dougal a look Poppy didn't miss that might have said something along the lines of "I'm in trouble."

Which, if the colonel chased after Anise, he was.

But, on the same note, Poppy very much wanted him to chase after her sister because that meant she and Dougal would be left alone. That her ravishment could begin, and she very much wanted her mouth on his.

The moment they'd started walking arm in arm along the Kyle, her limbs had thrummed with anticipation for a kiss they hadn't shared since the day before.

How funny that if she agreed to marry him—which she planned to do—she could kiss him whenever she wanted, but before they said, "I do," they had to sneak around? Though she supposed if they were in public or other people were around, they probably weren't supposed to show affection.

She had seen her mother and father kiss, but only when they didn't realize anyone was watching.

Dougal held out his hand to her. "I know the perfect spot."

Poppy didn't hesitate to put her hand in his, a spark of lightning flying up her arm the moment they touched, sending her entire body vibrating. Was he really going to ravish her in the garden? Did she want to be ravished?

She nearly laughed at this last question. She most certainly did.

Ahead in the garden, she could hear the charming sound of her sister's laugh, followed by the roar of the colonel's boisterous chuckle.

"They are having fun," Dougal said.

"Good, it will keep them occupied and not looking for us." Oh, how brazen she was and how very much she didn't care.

Dougal grinned and led her through the maze, twisting and turning, the sound of her sister and Colonel Austen growing fainter and fainter until they reached a wall covered in ivy and a dead end.

"Have you lost your way?" she asked.

"No' at all." He swept away the ivy, revealing a tiny latch, which he lifted and then pushed, the door creaking open to reveal a secret garden.

"Oh my," Poppy said as he led her through and shut the door behind them. All around her were various blooms, the fragrance mesmerizing. "This is so stunning."

"No' as stunning as ye." Dougal pulled her into his arms, and she followed his tug, pressing herself against him and leaning up on tiptoes to steal the kiss she'd been thinking about for hours.

Dougal's mouth brushed over hers, softly at first, then firmer, then downright primal as his tongue swept into her mouth to claim ownership.

She sighed into his kiss, her tongue dancing over his, her fingers curling against his shoulders. Every part of her body came alive with his kiss, tingles, heat and a voracious pulse between her thighs that begged to be satisfied.

They'd kissed before, several times now. Though the kisses that came between London and now seemed tame in comparison. Dougal wasn't holding anything back now, and she wasn't either. He'd promised her a ravishing, and she was getting his full and undivided attention.

"*Mo chreach*," he murmured that Gaelic expletive against her lips, but rather than be offended, she laughed.

"Bloody hell," she replied, smiling before she sucked at his tongue.

Dougal growled low in his throat, wrapped his arm around her waist and lifted her closer, pressing himself fully against her. His breeches did nothing to hide the evidence of his desire, long, hard and thick, his arousal pressed with passion against her midsection, and Poppy, who was an innocent still in most senses of the word, knew at once what it meant to be a hedonistic wanton. She rubbed against his arousal, gasping at the increase of thrumming between her thighs; the heat that needed and wanted his touch.

"Slow down," he murmured, panting. "I'm supposed to ravish ye, no' the other way around."

"I don't even know what I'm doing...just feeling," she confessed. "And it feels so good."

Dougal's head fell back, and he sucked in a breath. She watched his shoulders rising and lowering with his heavy breaths, and then he took her by the hand and led her toward the promised bench, only this one was a swing suspended from a tree, slowly rocking as they sat upon it.

Poppy leaned into Dougal, putting her legs over his thighs, and then she gasped as he took her bold move a step further and tugged her completely onto his lap, her bottom pressed to the hardness of his strong legs.

At the contact, Dougal let out a low groan. Not a second later, he pressed his hands on either side of her face, guiding her mouth to his. His kiss was demanding—pure, unadulterated passion.

Poppy attempted for only a split second to put her mind to rights as his kiss thoroughly explored every inch of her mouth, but why would she want to be rational when her entire being wanted to be as enraptured as he was? Her fingers trembled, and every swipe of his tongue, every brush of his lips, had her going mad with need, with thoughts of what allowing herself to be ravished meant.

In Dougal's arms, she was certain she'd never been happier. Nor more nervous. Angsty thoughts plucked at her desire the way a seamstress poked a hem, but she ignored them. Pushed those thoughts aside. He loved her. Wanted to marry her. This was what she wanted. Poppy raised a hand to his shoulder and squeezed the taut muscles beneath the fabric of his clothes.

Shivers raced up and down her spine and limbs, leaving tingles of anticipation. Her nipples grew taut, aching with need and sending frissons of pleasure to pull at her core. She shifted on his lap, pressing herself to his chest to feel the length of him, his warmth on her body beneath hers.

Her fingers trailed up to his neck, feeling the thrumming pulse under his skin.

DOUGAL WASTED NO TIME IN TAKING POSSESSION OF Poppy's offered mouth. They both let out sighs of satisfaction as the frenzy of their kiss turned to touching exploration. An urgency took hold of Dougal as he slid his hand up her thigh. He held her, pulled tight to him so he could feel every lush curve against him. Poppy was a goddess among women, her fingers stroking his hair and sending him to the heavens.

He hooked his hand underneath one of her knees, and Poppy shifted, wrapping her arms around his neck and then she shocked him by wrapping one leg around his hip.

Mo chreach!

He'd promised her a ravishing, and yet it seemed his temptress had taken the helm, ravishing him instead. Unable to help himself, he slid his hands beneath her bottom, pulled the other leg around his hip and held her like that, straddled against him on the rocking bench. The heat of her sex emanated through her gown to his breeches, making his already scorching blood burn hotter, his groin throbbing with the need to claim her fully.

Dougal needed to set some boundaries and put an end to this, or she was going to become his body and soul before they said, "I do."

Just this one indulgence. A kiss. A few touches. Her, rocking against him. All clothes left on.

Her lush breasts were crushed to his chest. He groaned at the softness of her curves surrounding him. Just a touch...he slid a hand over her ribs to cup a plush swell. Even through the fabric, he could feel the warmth of her skin and wanted to feel the weight of her naked, soft breast against his palm. Dougal rubbed a thumb over her nipple, reveling in her gasp, the soft inhale so sensual against his mouth.

Poppy scraped her fingernails along the back of his neck, massaged his shoulders and rocked her hips against his in a rhythm that made him think he'd died and gone to heaven. Her thighs were clenched tight around his hips, making him hard with need.

He had to stop now if he was going to. While he still had a thread of control left. He was very close to coming completely unraveled, shredding their clothes, and taking her on the ground of the walled-in garden. Dougal tried to take his lips from Poppy's, but she only leaned in closer and clutched harder, making him want to forget all his promises to save making love for their wedding night.

"Please, Dougal, let's not stop yet," she murmured, her words an enticing invitation.

How could he deny her? Or himself...

They'd begun this slow seduction in a garden hundreds of miles away a year ago. And he'd craved her ever since. Dougal wanted to give in to their desire, to throw caution to the wind. But he also knew that if he didn't put a halt to this rapturous encounter, it would end with Poppy pinned beneath him while he buried himself deep inside her hot, wet...

Even the images he conjured in his mind were too much to bear. Just one more little taste. He pulled her in for another heated kiss, feeling his way along her skirts until his hand was underneath. He skimmed his way from her silky calf to her smooth thigh.

Poppy whimpered and hugged him closer. Urged him to continue his exploration as his finger went higher, higher still, through the slit of her drawers and brushed the silky curls of her damp sex. Poppy cried out, and he groaned as he stroked, gentle and slow at first and then with quicker, firmer circles. Beneath his touch, she trembled.

"Dougal," she whispered.

He knew what she wanted, what she silently pleaded for. It was what he wanted for her too. For her to break apart. He stroked and caressed and kissed until her entire body convulsed, and he swallowed her cry of passion, kissing her until the quaking subsided.

As much as he wanted more, this had to be enough.

For now.

Dougal finally tore himself away. He lifted her from his lap, placed her on the bench and got down on his knees in front of her.

"Lass, I beg of ye, marry me. I canna go another day without knowing your sweet honey is mine."

"Bring me a priest, and I'll say, 'I do' right now," she teased, pinching his chin. "Though I think my mother would be disappointed at being left out of the ceremony."

"Soon then."

"Yes, very soon."

19

"Ladies, ladies," Mama practically yelped as she bustled into the drawing room, whipping off her bonnet, her cheeks pink as if she'd run all the way from her tea in town with a friend rather than taking the curricle.

"What's happened?" Poppy was immediately on edge. There had to have been some news. There could be no other reason for their mother's flurry and pitch. A war must have broken out somewhere. Or perhaps Mary had succumbed to a fever.

"The ladies in town are all agog with news from Edinburgh."

"Do tell us," Anise said, tossing her book aside in favor of gossip.

"Well, it would seem that a certain young lady who has been plaguing you, Poppy, has eloped, and there are rumors that she is..." Her mother inhaled and looked side to side, then got up and shut the drawing room door as if their servants might take this gossip and spread it wide. "That she is with child," she whispered.

Poppy's face colored at having already known this was possibly the case, given what Dougal had told her about Lucia and because what she'd done with him the day before could have nearly put her in the same position if they hadn't stopped when they did.

She was glad Dougal had the sense to hold back when she'd been willing to give him everything. Because Lucia was proof of what could happen when a man made promises and didn't keep them. Not that she would compare Dougal to Campbell at all, but one did need to protect themselves until the ring was on the finger.

"Did she elope with Campbell?" Poppy asked.

Her mother looked at her sharply. "How did you know?"

Poppy shrugged. "Lucky guess? I had heard they had an attachment previously."

"Well, it's true. They have eloped to Gretna Green and her father is beside himself."

Interesting they chose that iconic place to elope when in Scotland they could have gotten married anywhere.

"Is he? But why? If Campbell is the father of the child that she carries? He has done the honorable thing. I'd think her father would be ecstatic."

Mama shivered as if Poppy had said something truly heinous. "Maybe he's not the father."

"Oh," Anise frowned. "Then why would he elope with her?"

"Good point. He probably is the father." Mama made a moaning sound and flicked her fan harder.

"We needn't speculate on the father," Poppy said. "The good news is that Lucia has finally married, and it isn't to Dougal."

Anise grinned. "Is it too early for champagne?"

Their mother gasped. "Anise!"

"What?" she shrugged. "Aren't ladies allowed to celebrate good news? Dougal is free to marry Poppy."

Her mother turned her eagle eyes on Poppy now. "Has he asked? The two of you have been spending an awful lot of time together."

Poppy swallowed, remembering how he'd begged her to be his wife in the garden, down on his knees in front of her. Told her he couldn't go another day without knowing she was his... Dear heavens. Heat crept up from her chest, circling her neck before slapping against her cheeks. She had to look away briefly, afraid her face would tell all her secrets.

"He has." She was proud of herself for being able to say it without her voice cracking or without collapsing from how boneless she felt at the memories of their wicked and delicious embraces.

"Oh my, I think we definitely need champagne," Anise said again. "Two good news items in ten minutes? How could we not?"

"It is highly inappropriate," their mother said, flopping delicately on the sofa.

"Who would know besides us?" Anise argued.

Poppy nodded, imagining the bubbles might settle the sudden rapid beating of her heart. "She has a point."

"The servants would think us drunkards." Mama frowned.

Anise wiggled her brows. "Perhaps they'd like to join us."

"Oh no, no, no." Mama flopped again.

But they didn't have time to get the champagne or even offer a glass of anything to their servants as they heard the sounds of a rider outside the cottage.

"Who is that?" Mama asked, bounding toward the window with Poppy and Anise, her weakness suddenly gone. "Lord Reay." Her mother turned to look at Poppy. "Did you know he was coming?"

"I didn't." Though she'd hoped against hope.

"Everyone sit," Mama instructed. "Pretend to be busy doing whatever it is men think we do in drawing rooms besides gossip."

Anise grabbed her book. Mama opened her knitting basket. And Poppy, too stunned to do anything, stared at the door until there was a soft knock, and their Jack of all trades opened the door and announced Dougal's arrival.

Dougal stepped into the drawing room, his gaze immediately on Poppy. "Miss Featherstone," he murmured. "Lady Cullen, Miss Anise."

"Welcome," Poppy said, her brain suddenly a blank canvas and all words evaporating like steam on a bath. One look at Dougal, and she was melting where she stood, phantom memories of her legs wrapped around him, her mouth on his.

"If I might have a word with Miss Featherstone," he asked her mother.

"Oh, I think you can call her Poppy," her mother said with a slight laugh as if it were all very silly, but Poppy's nerves made her stomach do flips, and his use of formality made it worse, so she was grateful in fact for her mother's sudden departure of proper address.

"Yes," Poppy managed to say, standing on numb feet as she approached Dougal, who held out his elbow and led her outside the cottage. Beneath her fingers, the heat of his arm singed, and she grabbed hold tighter, not afraid to get burned.

They'd not made it ten feet beyond the door before he said, "There's been some news."

Her heart dropped, afraid now was when he'd let her down gently.

"About Lucia?" she asked with hope.

"Aye."

Poppy let out the breath she'd been holding. "I heard she's eloped."

He stopped walking, facing her with a grin that made his eyes sparkle. "Aye, she has."

"And that means you're free from your...what shall we call it? Your folly?"

He chuckled, and for a minute, she thought he was going to kiss her, but perhaps sensing that her mother and sister were most likely spying, he stopped. "I'd say I dodged a bullet, perhaps from her father's pistol at dawn." Dougal got down on his knees, and Poppy gasped.

"Oh, do get up," she pleaded. "They can all see you."

"Good. I want them to know that I am forever your servant. That I love ye from the bottom of my heart, and I would be honored if ye would agree to be my wife—again, formally. No' when we've...well, no' when we've just been in the garden. I want ye to be my life partner."

Poppy's heart seized somewhere behind her ribs, and then, as quickly as it stopped beating, it started up at an erratic pace. "On one condition," she whispered, her voice failing her, so thick was her throat with emotion.

"Anything."

"You promise to teach our sons never to make oaths to women, declarations of any kind, while under the influence of too many spirits."

"I promise, love, and I will also request they speak with their very intelligent mother before doing any such thing to make sure they are making the right decision."

Poppy felt as if she were floating on air with happiness. "I want any children we have to find love."

"I would never wish for anything less. So, do ye accept my proposal?"

"I have another condition."

"All ye need do is ask." The earnestness in his gaze, his tone, was enough to make her want to drop to her knees with him, but her mother would kill her if she dirtied her dress.

"I would like for you to give my dowry to my mother. She has not been left with much, and she has done so much for my sister and me."

Dougal nodded. "Done. And I will see to your mother's comfort and every need. She will want for nothing."

Tears stung Poppy's eyes, and she smiled. How the world had turned! And she was going to be the happiest of brides. "Then it is with much joy and hope that I accept."

Dougal stood then, wrapped her in his arms, and in front of her sister and mother, who were most definitely staring out the window—for she could hear their gasps—he kissed her.

"I love you, Dougal Mackay," she whispered against his mouth. "You stole my heart in London, and I feel as if you've now given it back tenfold."

"I would give ye anything ye asked for."

The front door of the cottage burst open, and Mama popped out with Anise on her heels.

"Do we have cause to celebrate?" Mama asked, her voice several octaves higher than usual.

"We do." Poppy gazed up at Dougal. "We are to be married."

Anise let out a squeal that scared off a few birds perched in the trees.

"Oh, my darling girl." Mama started to cry, holding out her arms, and Poppy rushed into them. "You did it, I am so happy for you."

There was more to her mother's emotion, her words, than simply being proud Poppy had finally made a match. It was a relief from the financial tightness she'd felt. The worry that they'd be able to make it on the small allowances they had.

A thousand pounds was ten times the annual income her mother was allowed from their father's estate, and she could use it however she wanted.

"Dougal." Her mother let go of Poppy and held her hand out to her future son-in-law, who took it, bending over to kiss the air above her knuckles. "Congratulations."

"I am a lucky man to have your daughter as a wife."

"She is a wonderful woman."

"I couldna agree more." He glanced at Poppy, his eyes sparkling with love and pride. "She has made me a verra happy man."

"I'm so glad for the two of you." Anise hugged Poppy to her and then hugged Dougal too.

He was startled at first and then leaned into the hug.

"There is something I would like to offer," Dougal said.

"But first, I think you were right, Anise, we need champagne." Mama hurried into the house to speak with their housekeeper, and the three of them followed her inside to the drawing room, where Jack was opening a bottle. "You were saying?"

"I know ye're verra partial to this cottage left to ye by your husband, but I wanted to offer ye the use of any of my houses at your leisure. There's no reason for ye to be in one place if ye dinna prefer it."

"Oh, Dougal, you are too kind, and that is too much to ask." Mama glanced around the room, a look of nostalgia crossing her features, and Poppy wondered if she were remembering a time she'd come here with her husband. "I find this cottage rather cozy."

"Mama," Poppy said, "Dougal is also going to give you my dowry to keep and spend as you like."

At this, her mother's face grew pale. "Oh, Poppy, you do

not need to do that. It is yours, given to you by your father. I cannot accept it."

Poppy glanced up at Dougal, who nodded encouragingly. "I know. And I am grateful to him for being so generous. But I am more than secure with Dougal. And I want you to have it. Papa would understand and agree with me, I'm sure."

"Oh, Poppy. I..." Her mother was suddenly overcome with emotion and excused herself.

"Oh, no." Poppy started to follow her mother, afraid she'd upset her, but Anise stood in her way.

"Let her go," her sister said softly with a smile. "She's not upset, just overcome. You've made her very happy. She has been quite stressed about how to get by, and you've just given her a huge gift. Both of you." Anise looked at Dougal and nodded.

Poppy hugged her sister. "Thank you."

"It is I who have you to thank." Anise wiggled her brows as if she had a secret.

"We will give ye a proper season too," Dougal said. "Ye deserve it."

"I'm not sure I need it." Anise bit her lower lip, then peeled off her glove to reveal a small sapphire ring.

"What is that?" Poppy reeled in shock.

"Colonel Austen gave it to me. He's asked me to marry him. I planned to tell you and Mama after she came back from tea, but then Dougal came and proposed."

"Both of us, married!" Poppy clapped her hands together.

"I'm so happy for us, for you," Anise said.

"And I am so happy for you and us."

Jack cleared his throat, and the sisters turned to see him still standing there with the champagne bottle.

"Oh yes, please, do pour," Poppy said. "So sorry to have forgotten."

Jack smiled. "No' a problem at all, miss. My congratulations to the lot of ye."

"Thank ye," Dougal said, taking two glasses of sparkling champagne and passing it to Poppy and Anise.

Mama took that moment to return, and he handed her a glass as well.

They were about to raise their glasses in a toast when a knock sounded at the front door.

"That must be the colonel," Anise said, passing Poppy her glass and rushing from the room.

She returned a moment later with Colonel Austen, who looked sheepishly at them all holding their champagne glasses.

"I see we have much to celebrate," he said.

"Indeed, we do"," Mama said, looking slightly puzzled, then finally noticing Anise's ring when her daughter wriggled her fingers in her direction. "What is that?"

"My lady," Colonel Austen said. "I have asked Anise to marry me."

Mama looked ready to faint, flicking open her fan once more out of habit, but Dougal took hold of her arm to keep her steady. "Two daughters married?"

Poppy was afraid she was going to rush out of the room in tears again, but she managed to stay put this time.

"Mama, the colonel is also giving you my dowry. We believe you deserve it and that Edward has done you wrong."

"Oh, let us not talk about Edward and Mary at this most celebratory moment."

But fate had other designs. At that moment, there was another knock at the door, and then the piercing voice of Mary in the small foyer outside the drawing room as she let herself in the house.

"What in the world?" Poppy, Anise and their mother said

at the same time as Dougal and the colonel muttered, "Bloody hell."

The drawing room door burst open. Mary, red-faced, her hair a little askew from what had to be a fast-paced journey from Edinburgh, stood there before them, glowering fire and brimstone.

"What's the meaning of this?" she asked, staring each of them down as if they were schoolchildren who'd hidden the teacher's books.

For a moment, Poppy stood shocked, imagining that Mary had somehow gained magical powers. That in her finely appointed drawing room in Edinburgh, she'd heard Dougal declare himself for her and that she'd snapped her fingers and appeared.

"I beg your pardon, Mary, but that is no way to enter your mother-in-law's home." Mama's voice was stern, and for the first time that Poppy had ever seen, her mother looked down her nose at her daughter-in-law with an expression that would have put Poppy in the corner.

"Why, I never—" Mary started.

But this time, it was Poppy who stepped in. "How lovely to see you. What brings you to the Highlands?" She tried to keep her voice pleasant, but she feared the brittle smile on her face wasn't helping.

Mary ignored her. "Dougal. Lucia has eloped with Campbell, and when I arrived at Castle Varrich, they told me I could find you here. And now I see the lot of you drinking champagne in the middle of the day." This last part, she said as if she'd found them all drunk on whisky at breakfast.

"We have much to celebrate," Dougal said. "I have asked Poppy to marry me. And Anise and Colonel Austen have also gotten engaged."

Mary's mouth fell open as she stared from one of them to the next, clearly shocked.

"What about Lucia?"

"I was never meant to marry her. And as ye mentioned, she's properly wed to another. Now, let us no' bring up such unpleasantness. Do ye no' want to wish my fiancée your felicitations?" Dougal said brightly.

Mary visibly gritted her teeth, clearly having a lot of things to say, but either unwilling or unable to voice them. At last, she sniffed and held her nose in the air. "Well, I do hope you're all happy with yourselves."

It wasn't so much a congratulation as an accusation, as if they'd done something to hurt her, which they hadn't.

"Mary, our happiness doesna take away from yours." Dougal's voice was calm as he said it, and Mary remained stiff even as he pulled her into his arms for a one-sided hug, her arms hanging like two steel bars at her sides.

Was that the root of it, then? That Mary thought their happiness would somehow dip into her own? It was silly and irrational, but it also made sense. Mary didn't see the world in the same way as anyone else. She didn't see people outside of herself, autonomous. Everything that happened in the world was happening to her, or somehow, in her mind, she believed it affected her.

"I'm so very happy to have you as a sister-in-law times two," Poppy said, taking Dougal's place in hugging the cold stiffness that was Mary's body. My goodness, was she this way with Edward? No wonder she wasn't happy.

"That is," Mary swallowed and grimaced at the same time as if she were swallowing bile but would rather toss up her accounts. "That is a fact."

Poppy held in her laugh. How hard it was for Mary to compliment anyone.

"I'd best be returning to Edinburgh," Mary said.

"Ye've just arrived. Why no' share some champagne and then go back to the castle with me?" Dougal said. "We'll send a messenger to retrieve Edward, and the two of ye can be here for the wedding."

Mary shook her head so vehemently that more hair came out of her usually tight chignon. "I don't think that's a good idea. Edward is so busy."

"Then ye stay for the wedding." Dougal's expression suggested she not argue. "I'd like to have someone from my family there, and Mary, ye're the only sister I've got."

Mary's smile was sickly. "I supposed Edward is probably not that busy. But no champagne for me. I'll return to Varrich and have a messenger sent."

"Are you certain, dear? It's quite delicious," Mama said, holding out a glass.

Mary gave their mother a look that said she'd rather have her skin peeled off. "Ladies shouldn't."

One last little dig before she went.

"Sometimes, ladies should," Anise said with a shrug.

Before Mary could start another argument, Poppy took her arm. "I'll walk you out. What flowers do you think would be the best for the wedding?"

Mary at first looked stunned, then delighted to be asked her opinion. After all, she had an opinion on everything and was always right, at least in her mind. If that was what it took to get her excited and not combative, then Poppy was willing to defer to her for all floral decisions.

"I think myrtle, lily of the valley, a thistle and some white roses."

"That sounds lovely."

"It does. And Castle Varrich has its own botanical greenhouse."

"I do remember seeing something like that when I was there." Poppy bit the inside of her cheek as she recalled exactly where she'd seen them.

"I'll see if we've got the right flowers," Mary said, taking ownership of the greenhouse.

Poppy wasn't going to take the bait if that was what it was. Mary had grown up going to Castle Varrich, and really had more ownership to it as far as memories were concerned, though the secret garden where Dougal had given such pleasure...well, that she would fight for.

She glanced over her shoulder at Dougal, who still stood in the drawing room, his gaze on her, and the way he looked at her made her body flush. Saints, but she loved that man so much, and to think that after trying to forget him for nearly a year, all of her dreams were coming true.

🦋 20 🦋

The wedding ceremony and the feast were over before Poppy could blink. She barely noticed the nasty looks and snarky comments from Mary. She smiled but hardly heard any congratulations from her mother and friends. All she could think about was what was going to happen after the ceremony.

What was going to happen right now.

They stood in Dougal's bedroom in the medieval castle that had housed Mackays for generations. The wood of the floorboards was cool beneath her bare feet; her shoes were the only thing she'd removed.

"Ye are stunning." Dougal stared at her the way he'd been doing since he'd first seen her that afternoon. A hungry, primal look in his eyes. The same one she'd seen in the garden.

One that mirrored her own hunger for his embrace.

Before she could respond to his compliment—though to be fair, she was having a hard time forming sentences—he moved closer, stroked his hand over her cheek, then leaned down and did the most delicious thing. He licked her lower lip, tugged it gently with his teeth.

Poppy sighed, stunned and excited all at once. Frissons of hot desire fired, pooling at her center, and her knees felt suddenly weak. This was the moment she'd been waiting for. When they could officially strip each other bare...

All pretense was gone. He loved her. She loved him.

They were wedded, and now it was time to get bedded.

Poppy wanted to make Dougal as weak in the knees as she was. She captured his tongue between her teeth and sucked it into her mouth. He growled, a deep, vibrating noise that caused the place between her thighs—the place he'd kissed—to pulse.

"Ye vixen," he crooned against her mouth, and she couldn't help but smile.

Dougal stroked a sizzling path with the backs of his fingers up her arms, singeing her skin through the fabric of her gown.

He gently massaged her shoulders, her back, the sides of her ribs. And then the moment she'd been waiting for: his fingers brushed the undersides of her breasts. If she'd had the strength to do it, she would rip this bloody wedding gown from her body. The fantasy of touching her bare skin to his was real. So very real.

Her nipples hardened into taut, aching buds that begged for his touch, but he didn't go near them. Instead, he drove her mad by stroking everywhere else. Dougal was good at teasing...too good. They'd barely gotten into their room, this being only their second kiss as a wedded couple—and really, the brief kiss at the altar was nothing compared to this—and already she was melting in a puddle of desire and need.

The need to touch skin to skin was overwhelming.

Poppy gently broke their kiss and took a step back. Dougal looked puzzled at first, but then she smiled and turned around, peeking at him over her shoulder.

"Unbutton me, husband."

Dougal's eyes widened, then grew heavy. His chest rose and fell as he drew in and let out a deep breath, nearly a low whistle.

In less than a heartbeat, Dougal closed the distance between them. His fingers, steadier than her own, plucked at the buttons along her spine until her dress was fully undone.

Poppy slid a hand under the fabric at her shoulder and peeled it down her arm, but before she could reach the other side, Dougal saw to it; the scrape of his calloused palm on her bare shoulder sent shivers rushing through her.

The gown fell to her feet, and she kicked it aside in a pool of fabric. Then she turned back around, still dressed in her thin chemise. Dougal raked his eyes over her, and she realized, as she never had before, how threadbare it was, that her hardened nipples pressed against the fabric, each rosy circle visible. Dougal swallowed hard enough for her to hear, his gaze riveted to the spot. Poppy's breath quickened, and she grew suddenly bolder, arching her back slightly as she took hold of the ribbons at the center of her chest.

"Wait," Dougal said, his voice low and gravelly. "Allow me to do it."

Poppy stilled her fingers, and he took her hand, pressing his lips to her knuckles as his other hand took hold of the ribbons between his thumb and forefinger. He tugged unhurriedly, the sound of the silky ribbons swishing as they loosened echoing in the bedroom.

Heart pounding, skin prickling with anticipation, Poppy found it hard to draw a breath. Her chemise fell apart nearly to her navel, exposing the expanse of her breasts and her abdomen. The cool air made her nipples even harder, but there was no mistaking that the tingling she felt was from Dougal's gaze and the desire for his touch.

"Ye're even more beautiful than I imagined," he said.

His compliment gave her confidence, and she dipped one shoulder and then the other until the fabric slipped away, whispering down her legs to her ankles, leaving her fully naked.

Dougal sucked in a ragged breath, then reached for her, running his fingers

from her cheek down to the dip in her throat, then lower through the valley of her breasts until he stopped at her navel.

Her skin pebbled everywhere he touched, and she shivered.

"Saints," he said under his breath.

"Touch me more." The demand was out before she could pull it back—before she' realized what she had said.

"As ye wish, my love." He leaned forward and pressed his warm lips to her collarbone, leaving a trail of heat as he slipped his lips along the length of that bone, over her chest, and then down between her breasts. His hands followed the same path until he was cupping her breasts, his hot breath on her skin.

"Please," she whimpered, desperately wanting him to touch his tongue to her nipple.

Dougal didn't disappoint, flicking his tongue out to taste and devouring her. She sighed, then moaned, her fingers finding an anchor in his shoulders so she didn't fall over from the exquisite torment of his deliciously wicked tongue. Though she protested, he kissed his way back up to her mouth, making her eager for more—of everything.

Dougal pulled her taut against him, hands wrapped

around her waist, and claimed her mouth in a heated, possessive kiss. His scent surrounded her in a cloud of spicy maleness. Intoxicating.

All the gentleness of before was gone, replaced by something feral, primal. Their tongues melded and stroked in a frenzy as if, at any moment, they might wake from a dream, and neither of them wanted to miss a moment.

Poppy gripped the buttons of his jacket, tugging them free, hearing the distinct plink of one of them hitting the floor.

Oops...

Dougal tore his jacket from his body, his mouth still on hers, and then his shirt, which meant he did have to break away, but only for a second. And when he had tossed the fabric aside, Poppy splayed her hands on the bare, hard muscles surrounding his spine, then wrapped her arms around to his chest. He was warm, brawny—pure strength.

She stared in awe at the beautiful formation of his body. So different from her own. So masculine. Something inside her sparked, igniting into a frenzied fire. When she glanced up at him, Dougal's eyes matched her passion. He claimed her mouth once more with thrilling force. The power and passion behind his kiss made her tremble and soar at the same time.

She crushed her breasts to his chest, feeling the spark of lightning at the clash. Exhilarating to finally touch so intimately. They explored each other with frenzied hands, hungry to know every plane and divot. Anticipation and excitement filled her, consumed her. Dougal knew how to touch her to make her sigh and moan. Every caress, every kiss, had her feeling boneless, breathless.

Poppy skimmed her fingers over the waistband of his breeches, and Dougal hissed a breath against her lips.

"Och, lass..." he growled, giving her lower lip a gentle nip.

Wherever his lips touched, she burned. Wherever his fingers grazed, she felt thrilled. And from how he breathed, the slight tremble in his hands, she was sure he felt the same way.

Growing bolder in her exploration, Poppy pressed her lips to Dougal's corded neck. He hissed again, emboldening her. She licked a path from his neck to his shoulder. As if in competition with who could tease who, he too grew more frenzied, licking at her flesh. She mirrored his every move, her tongue darting over his salty skin, then sucking until he gasped.

But then Dougal won their little competition as he cupped her breasts once more. Poppy gasped and thrust her chest forward, filling his hands more fully. His touch was warm, and yet she shivered. Dougal's hot breath caressed over her flesh, and she whimpered. Wanted him to taste her nipples again. To feel that delicious thrill. She never wanted him to stop.

Searing hot velvet touched a taut nipple, and Poppy moaned. Her eyes sank closed in ecstasy as his tongue flicked over her nipple. My god, but he was magic with his mouth. Molten magic.

She gripped the back of his head, threading her fingers into his hair and holding him in place. Dougal chuckled, undulating his tongue in decadent caresses again and again until the exquisite pleasure of it was almost too much.

With trembling fingers, Poppy explored Dougal's chest, his abdomen, feeling the flex of his muscles beneath her touch. Again, she skimmed her fingers around his waistband and beneath it. If she was naked, he should be too.

"Take these off," she whispered. "Please."

Dougal gazed at her, his eyes hooded, his mouth curling into a wicked grin.

"What the lady wants, the lady gets." Dougal flicked open the buttons of his breeches, revealing more of his skin, and then...

Poppy rocked back on her heels and watched as he revealed a sprinkling of dark hair and a long, thick shaft—his arousal, the hardness that pressed to her and made her shiver. Her breath caught, and she felt slightly light-headed. Dougal was beyond striking. He was mesmerizing. Almost as if the heavens had opened up and sculpted him from the stones that jutted from the mountains.

For a few brief seconds, she was a little scared, but not in a terrifying way; more like, was she going to be any good at this? Without thinking, she reached out and skimmed her hand over his hard length, marveling at the velvet softness that was in contrast to the hardness beneath.

"Your skin is soft. I'd thought it would be... I don't know. Rougher somehow," she said with wonderment.

"Och, ye'll have me undone," he growled, then pressed his mouth to hers, their naked bodies clashing together in a heated, passionate friction.

Dougal slid his hand over her buttocks, and she whimpered as he tugged her even closer. The hardness of him pressing to the very heat of her and sending longing pulsing deep inside her core. He caressed her hip and tickled his way over her ribs to her breasts. Stroked her nipples while he devoured her mouth.

Dougal slipped his hand down her belly and between her thighs. She moaned when he slid a finger through her folds and stroked over the hardened, slick nub of her pleasure. Every part of her trembled. She arched into him, wanting more of the breathtaking sensations he gave her.

Then he pushed a finger inside her. Poppy cried out as her body convulsed, her sex clenching around his finger, knees growing weak. Just as she was about to collapse, Dougal lifted her into the air and carried her to the bed.

DOUGAL SMILED DOWN AT HIS WIFE AND THE WAY SHE WAS splayed out on the bed. A feast for the taking. How had he gotten so lucky? He was still in a semi-state of shock that she was his. That he'd been able to fix the near disaster of her disappearing from his life forever.

"I love ye," he said, and even those three little words did little to relay the scope and depth of his feelings for her.

He had to show her.

"I love you, too, husband."

Dougal lay on the bed beside her, tugging Poppy into his arms as he kissed her. She sighed into his mouth, the sound filled with the same pleasure and contentment he also felt. He loved the sounds she made when he touched her. Needed to hear more. He nuzzled a path between her breasts and kissed the soft planes of her belly. Stroked over the length of her thighs, running his hands from her knees to her hips and back.

"Poppy, ye're so beautiful," he whispered.

At his gentle nudging, she opened her thighs, revealing the glistening folds of her sex covered with a sprinkle of curls. Dougal's breath caught at the sight. Not as if he hadn't seen a woman naked before. But Poppy...his wife...his forever made this moment all the more powerful. He glanced at her face. Her eyes were heavily lidded, cloudy with desire, and she watched him, studied him. This woman, his wife, was *his*. And he was hers.

The moment he took her, and they consummated this

marriage, there was no going back. Not that he had plans to do so, but maybe she—

"Am I...still beautiful?" she asked. "For I have shocked you into silence."

His chest grew tight, and every muscle coiled, ready to spring. He made a vow to himself that he would make her cry out with pleasure again and again.

"Ye're everything I've ever wanted and more. The most beautiful woman I have ever beheld and I love ye more with every second that passes."

Dougal moved to kneel between her thighs, feeling the warm length of her strong legs on the outside of his thighs. His cock pulsed, blood surging into the length, making him rock-solid. Poppy's eyes riveted to him, sliding up and down his body with the same hunger careening through him.

He leaned down, his weight on an elbow. The heat of her sex cradled his shaft, and he groaned with pleasure. He laid claim with a kiss, unable to keep his mouth from hers any longer. At first, he thought to distract himself from what he wanted, which was to bury himself deep inside her, but this kiss... Her kiss did anything but distract. It only made him want her more. With their bodies pressed tight, all he had to do was shift an inch or two, and then he'd be notched and ready to drive home.

Tremors passed through him as she stroked a path up and down his back, gripping his shoulders, her thighs tightening at his hips. Making love to Poppy was turning out to be a whole new experience. Perhaps love did that. Perhaps it was Poppy herself.

One thing he was certain of was that he couldn't go on like this, or he was liable to lose all control. He needed her to find her pleasure before he got to the breaking point, and there was one way he knew she would enjoy.

Dougal kissed his way down her body, nudged her thighs apart when she tried to close them and gave a subtle shake of his head. "I'm going to taste ye, love."

And then he did, lowering himself to her delicious softness. Poppy gasped and clenched her thighs, her hands fisting in his hair.

Dougal teased, probed, licked, sucked. Poppy's soft whimpers grew to full-out cries of pleasure. With his thumbs, he opened her more, tasting, devouring. God, she was Heaven. Wet heat and feminine decadence. He suckled the taut nub of flesh that pulsed and flicked his tongue over it again and again, making love to her with his mouth.

Poppy's thighs shook, and she clenched tighter, lifting her hips higher. From her pants and moans, he sensed she was close, and Dougal increased his pace.

She cried out as her body broke apart in a climax that had her quaking against him, thighs clenching, legs shaking.

Dougal grinned. "I love watching ye find your pleasure."

"And you're so...good at giving it to me."

Dougal chuckled as he slid up her body until their lips were touching once more. "I'm going to give ye more."

"I want all of you." Poppy lifted her thighs around his hips, her hands dancing up his arms.

Dougal tilted his hips, notching his cock at the entrance of her slick heat.

"This may pinch," he said.

"I know. I'm not scared."

"I'm sorry," he said as he inched his way slowly inside her exquisitely tight channel.

Poppy didn't cry out in pain, but she stiffened as he went. He kissed her, stroked her, trying to ease the discomfort of his passage until he was fully inside her, surrounded by her snug heat.

"Are ye all right?" His voice came out a croak as he gazed down at her, trying to judge how she felt. At the same time, he tried not to breathe, knowing if he wasn't careful, he was one thrust away from the release of his life.

"I'm fine, better than fine," she murmured, moving to kiss him.

That was all the reassurance he needed. He claimed her mouth, kissing her with deep promise. He didn't withdraw right away but rather pressed and pressed, rotating his hips to try and spark pleasure from her, to get her used to his girth.

When she responded eagerly, tilting her hips into his, Dougal withdrew, then eased back inside with torturous slowness. Poppy moaned with pleasure, her nails digging into his back, and he withdrew again, only this time he plunged back inside, some of the control he had slipping. He had wanted to go slow. Wanted to make their pleasure last... But her enthusiasm and his desire won out.

He gritted his teeth and charged ahead, thrusting over and over, her body clenching around his. A climax was on the brink of her horizon.

"Oh, Dougal," she gasped. "I think... Oh!"

She convulsed beneath him, and he was lost. Pleasure radiated from the base of his spine and surged outward in a powerful explosion of the most exquisite rapture, and he let out a growl that echoed in the ancient bedchamber.

Dougal collapsed against her, then rolled to the side, pulling her with him. His breaths came in hard pants, and his mind raced from what had happened. He'd made love dozens, hundreds of times. But this...this had been earth-shattering.

"Poppy." He kissed her lightly on the shoulders, then her lips.

"Dougal."

"Did I hurt ye?"

"Quite the opposite. I want to do it again."

Dougal grinned. "I am happy to do it as many times as ye like."

"Good. Because I have a feeling, I'll not want to leave this bedchamber for at least a week."

Then she shoved him on his back and climbed over top of him.

EPILOGUE

Several months later...

"Oh, my darling, how I have missed this delicious iced cream." Poppy let out a contented sigh in the creamery in Edinburgh. They'd not been back to the city since they'd gotten married, and this had been one of the first places she'd wanted to stop.

The last few weeks, she'd had an incredible craving for the treat, day and night.

"Anything for ye, my love." Dougal sat across from her, staring at her the same way he had the very first time they'd come here months ago.

Now, having been fully introduced to what a look like that meant, her insides thrummed, especially between her thighs.

"Perhaps we ought to skip the ball later," he suggested.

"Oh, we simply cannot." She licked her spoon, and Dougal's eyes widened.

"I beg of ye." He leaned forward, his knee pressing hers

from beneath the table, and his fingers brushed over her thigh.

Poppy glanced around, afraid someone might see him touching her so intimately, but no one seemed to notice.

"How about a long afternoon nap?" she offered suggestively.

"I accept."

Poppy grinned at her husband and took another lick of her spoon. "Ava has worked so hard on this event, and I'd hate to miss it."

"'Tis a matchmaking ball," Dougal responded. "What good is it for us to go?"

"Because she promised her father she was done with matchmaking. Some couples have to be there, or else he'll see right through her ruse."

Dougal chuckled. "I think he'll see right through it anyway."

"Perhaps. But if I do recall, Ava can be very convincing."

"Alas, she has convinced ye to come to her silly ball."

"This is true. But I promise your friends will be there, including Baron Darkwood, and so you, too, shall have a good time."

Dougal chuckled. "Darkwood? I'll believe it when I see it. From what I understand, he has had quite a row with the residents of Heatherfield."

"Ava's father?"

Dougal smiled and leaned forward conspiratorially, his fingers inching up her thigh. "In fact, nay, my love. I do believe he has an issue with the lady herself."

"Oh!" Poppy's interest grew. "Do you think we might witness a scandal this evening?"

"There's a real chance, and I'll say I'm a wee bit more

interested in attending now if only to watch Darkwood attempt to hold himself together."

"He's temperamental?"

"No' exactly." Dougal's grin widened. "I've only ever seen him miffed when he speaks of Lady Ava. Colonel Austen can attest to it."

"Fascinating. Austen and Anise will also be in attendance. I can't wait to see my sister; her letters from her honeymoon in France were so entertaining."

"Another reason we will be sure to attend. I'd no' want ye to miss the happy reunion with your sister."

Poppy grinned and took another spoonful of her frozen chocolate, letting it melt slowly on her tongue. "Perhaps we should make certain to arrive right on time. I know you prefer a later entrance to these things, as do I, but tonight is looking very promising."

Dougal pouted as if she'd taken away his iced cream. "I was promised a *nap*." The way he said it and how his eyes skimmed down to her mouth had Poppy squirming in her chair with anticipation. No longer was it the iced cream she was craving.

"Oh, you shall have your nap, husband." She ran a foot up his calf. "I think we can manage both a lengthy nap and an entertaining evening of people-watching and catching up."

"Have I told ye lately how much I love ye?" He seized her foot before she reached his tender parts.

"Indeed, you have," she teased. "Now, let us leave so I can show you how much I love you too."

Dougal stood so abruptly from his chair that it teetered on its back legs, which he quickly righted, excusing himself to the startled guests.

They didn't make it halfway down the road before they took their *nap* in the carriage.

Thank you for reading **A DASH OF SCOT**! I hope you loved Bryson and Freya's love story as much as I do. I'm a total sucker for a Pride and Prejudice theme. Guess what? There's more to come! Bryson and Freya will make cameo appearances in the next books in the series. Coming up next will be a Dash of Scot, available now for preorder.

BUT YOU DON'T HAVE TO WAIT TO READ MORE EXCITING REGENCY SCOTS!

GET YOUR COPY OF RETURN OF THE SCOT! BOOK One in the Scots of Honor series.

SIGN UP FOR ELIZA KNIGHT'S NEWSLETTER: HTTPS:// elizaknight.com/newsletter/

You don't have to stop here! You can read ALL FOUR of the SCOTS OF HONOR books now!

Highland war heroes rebuilding their lives grapple with ladies forging their own paths—who will win?

Regency Scotland comes alive in the vibrant and sexy new SCOTS OF HONOR series by USA Today bestselling author Eliza Knight. Scottish military heroes, who want nothing more than to lay low after the ravages of war in 19th century France, find their Highland homecomings vastly contradict their simple desires. Especially when they meet the feisty lasses who are tenacious enough to take them on, and show them just what they've been missing out of life. In battle they can't be beaten, but in love, they all find the ultimate surrender.

Return of the Scot
The Scot is Hers
Taming the Scot
The Scot Who Loved Her

CAN'T GET ENOUGH SCOTTISH ROMANCE NOVELS BY ELIZA? Check out her Stolen Bride Series!

The Highlander's Temptation
The Highlander's Reward
The Highlander's Conquest
The Highlander's Lady
The Highlander's Warrior Bride
The Highlander's Triumph
The Highlander's Sin
Wild Highland Mistletoe (a Stolen Bride winter novella)
The Highlander's Charm (a Stolen Bride novella)
A Kilted Christmas Wish – a contemporary Holiday spin-off

HOW ABOUT SOME FIERCE HIGHLAND REBELS? CHECK OUT Eliza's Prince Charlie's Angels series!

The Rebel Wears Plaid
Truly Madly Plaid
You've Got Plaid

ABOUT THE AUTHOR

Eliza Knight is an award-winning and USA Today bestselling author.

Her love of history began as a young girl when she traipsed the halls of Versailles and ran through the fields in Southern France. She can still remember standing before the great golden palace, and imagining what life must have been like. Join Eliza (sometimes as E.) on riveting historical journeys that cross landscapes around the world.

While not reading, writing or researching for her latest book, she chases after her three children. In her spare time (if there is such a thing...) she likes daydreaming, wine-tasting, traveling, hiking, staring at the stars, watching movies, shopping and visiting with family and friends.

She is the creator of the popular historical blog, History Undressed and host on the History, Books and Wine podcast.

She lives in the Sunshine State with her own knight in shining armor, three princesses, two very naughty Newfies, and a turtle named Fish.

Visit Eliza at http://www.elizaknight.com or her historical blog History Undressed: www.historyundressed.com. Sign up for her newsletter to get news about books, events, contests and sneak peaks: https://elizaknight.com/news/!

facebook.com/elizaknightfiction

x.com/elizaknight

instagram.com/elizaknightfiction

bookbub.com/authors/eliza-knight

goodreads.com/elizaknight

Milton Keynes UK
Ingram Content Group UK Ltd.
UKHW031115080824
446563UK00001B/27